A COMFORTING KISS

"Miss Palmer? Elinor, has something upset you?"

Was she upset? Of course not. Her whole life was disintegrating, but the intrepid Elinor Richards was not upset.

"No, my lord." She managed to keep her voice calm. "I was merely indulging in a moment of self-pity."

"Somehow that does not seem in character for you." Without invitation, he sat next to her and put an arm around her shoulder in a friendly gesture. "If there is anything I can do, you've only to ask, you know."

"Th-thank you, my lord." She wanted to nestle into the warmth of his encircling arm, but steeled herself against doing so. She wiped her eyes with the back of her hand in a childlike gesture. "I'll be all right. You must not concern yourself."

"I thought we agreed on 'Elinor' and 'Adrian' in private," he said softly. He lifted her chin and forced her to look at him. The expression in his eyes deepened with compassion—and something else. "Please let me help," he whispered.

He held her gaze for a long moment. Sympathy, questioning, a degree of pain shone in his eyes. Then with a soft groan, he lowered his mouth to hers. . . .

Books by Wilma Counts

WILLED TO WED
MY LADY GOVERNESS

Published by Zebra Books

MY LADY GOVERNESS

Wilma Counts

Zebra Books
Kensington Publishing Corp.
http://www.zebrabooks.com

ZEBRA BOOKS are published by

Kensington Publishing Corp.
850 Third Avenue
New York, NY 10022

First Printing: January, 2000
10 9 8 7 6 5 4 3 2 1

Printed in the United States of America

For Bill and Dottie and John,
who *also* know what friendship is all about.

One

"I tell you, Ellie, I heard the two of them talking in the stable. They didn't know I was in Jupiter's stall. Uncle Brompton is planning to turn old Chicken Legs loose on you."

Lady Elinor Richards noted the anxiety in her brother's voice.

"You must not be disrespectful, Peter," she said automatically, trying to calm the young man as much as correct his all-too-accurate description of their uncle's unattractive friend. "Now tell me exactly what you heard."

"I don't remember the *exact* words, but Uncle said he would get the housekeeper's key to your chamber. Baron Pennington will enter your room and then Uncle will rouse the other guests and you'll be compromised. He said you'd have no choice but to marry the baron once Lady Hempton noised the word around the *ton*."

"So *that* was the reason for our rather odd assortment of house guests," she said. "I knew Uncle Brompton had something afoot. He was most unhappy when I refused the baron's offer."

This last was an understatement. Her uncle had been furious, threatening to lock her in her room until she came to her senses. She, in turn, had threatened to acquaint society with his behavior and his creditors with a true accounting of his finances. The old reprobate had backed down.

Now, however, he had come up with a frightening scheme to achieve his goal.

"Never mind, Peter," she said with more assurance than she felt. "I have expected something like this. Uncle Martin has become more and more insistent that I marry Pennington."

"Because Pennington has agreed to give him half your fortune once you're tied right and tight," her brother asserted. "I heard that, too."

"Is that it? I knew it had to do with Uncle's wanting to get his hands on my money, for lord knows Pennington really does have enough of his own."

"A fortune the size of yours ain't nothing to whistle away, though. What can you do? You are a year away from being five and twenty."

"I know. I will just have to find a way to hide until I can control my fortune myself. The trust is set up so that the only way he could possibly touch those funds would be through such an accomplice as he's chosen."

"Hide? What do you mean, hide?"

"If I am not here, they can hardly force me to the altar, can they?"

"Ellie! This is serious. You're not planning one of your harebrained schemes, are you?" Peter's tone sounded more like their late father's than that of a youngster of only fifteen years. "You remember what happened when you tried to make that frisky mare jump the stile."

"I remember." She touched her head where the bump had been.

"So, what are you planning then?"

"I'll not tell you more than I must, Peter. That way you will not have to lie outrageously. I shall disappear for a while, but I will write you once you return to school, so you are not to worry. You are not to try to contact me, either. Is that clear?"

"I don't like it. I don't like it at all."

"I know," she said, placating him, "but I must do this. I have some money of my own saved from last quarter's allowance, but I shall need all you can spare as well. Also, some of your clothing."

Elinor considered the guests milling about in the drawing room that now technically belonged to her brother Peter, the new Earl of Ostwick. However, she thought, a stranger happening on this scene would assume Uncle Brompton and his avaricious wife were the lord and lady of the manor.

When he drew up his will over a decade ago the previous earl had inexplicably named his only sister's husband guardian to his two children. In the intervening years, he had apparently forgotten that he had done so. Elinor had been traveling in Italy when her father died. Martin Brompton had lost no time establishing himself as head of the household, especially since the new earl was a schoolboy away at Eton most of the year. By the time Elinor returned, a new regime had been firmly installed.

She had tried to reassert the pattern of living at Ostwick Manor that she and Peter had known in previous years, but she was constrained by the fact that her uncle now gave the orders. Moreover, he not only had control of household accounts, he had also contrived to have most of the old familiar servants dismissed in her absence. He had once even denied her access to the stables to punish her for what he termed her "lack of cooperation." Still mourning her father, Elinor had refused to lend her presence to her aunt's proposal that they partake of the entertainments offered in London. Then there had been the matter of the Bromptons' pressing Baron Pennington's suit.

Pennington was five years older than her father would

have been. Balding and wearing an ill-fitting wig, he was a relic of a previous generation. His watery blue eyes seemed always to be stripping away her clothing layer by layer. He had a pot belly and spindly legs on which his stockings forever wrinkled. Once the man had caught her alone in the hall and tried to kiss her. His breath had been foul.

Undiscouraged by her polite but firm refusal, he had continued his suit through his friend, her uncle. Now Brompton and his wife had assembled this interesting collection of people, mostly hangers-on with the *ton*. Few of them were readily welcomed in the most select homes, but neither were they totally unacceptable. Elinor knew that more than one of her aunt's chosen guests used gossip as an *entre* to society.

The seating plan at dinner tonight had again placed Elinor next to the baron, but this time she was ready for him. Last night when his hand had surreptitiously strayed to her knee, she had pointedly removed it and twisted her legs as far away from him as possible.

Tonight when he attempted the same familiarity, she jabbed a hat pin into the back of his hand. He gasped, but recovered himself and quickly jerked his hand away.

"You vixen," he muttered, bending toward her. "You are long overdue for a few lessons in decorum."

"Perhaps. But I doubt you could qualify to teach such," she replied in a low voice and smiled blandly.

"We shall see." He turned his attention to the roast beef on his plate. She suspected from her uncle's angry glare that he had an idea of what had just transpired.

Not long after the gentlemen rejoined the ladies in the drawing room later, Elinor excused herself, pleading a headache. As she did she saw her uncle and the baron exchange a knowing look.

* * *

Before going down for dinner, she had packed a small bag with the plainest of her gowns and other essentials. Now she hastily dressed in the clothing her brother had secured for her, first winding a cloth tightly over her too-generous breasts to try to give herself a more masculine outline. An unfashionably large coat would serve to conceal her feminine waist. She pinned up her shoulder-length chestnut locks. A large floppy hat—also decidedly unfashionable—and serviceable boots completed her transformation from an elegant lady of the *ton* to a nondescript country lad.

After checking to see that she had the hall to herself, Elinor made her way carefully down the back stairs. She was certain the servants would be occupied elsewhere, but she breathed a sigh of relief when she was outside, having encountered no one.

Peter was waiting for her behind the stable with a saddled horse.

"Did anyone see you?" she asked, her voice low.

"No. The servants were all at their supper when I came out."

She secured the bag to the saddle and hugged Peter briefly before he gave her a hand to hoist herself astride the horse. It was not the first time she had ridden astride, but it felt strange all the same.

"I will turn her loose to find her way home later." She patted the mare's neck.

"Be careful, Ellie." Peter's eyes seemed unusually bright in the muted illumination of a clear summer evening.

"Good-bye, Peter. I'll be all right. I promise."

She rode for what she thought to be three or four hours, allowing the mare to pick her way carefully in country lanes and leaving the paths whenever any other traffic seemed in the offing. Sometime in the hours before dawn, she knew she was on the outskirts of Upper Netherford, a village some distance from Ostwick Manor. She turned the horse loose and settled herself under a huge elm to await daylight and the arrival of a public coach at the inn nearby. She was cold and uncomfortable, but to seek shelter at such an hour would attract undue attention.

The coach journey was relatively uneventful. She avoided others at stops and feigned sleep much of the time in the coach. There had been only one incident that threatened to undo her. She nearly dissolved into a fit of giggles when a young lady traveling with her mama had flirted outrageously with the young "man" in the opposite seat, casting him exaggeratedly seductive glances despite a stern reprimand from her long-suffering parent.

Two days later, Lady Elinor Richards was sipping tea in London with her former governess.

Miss Harriet Palmer, who would have been surprised to find any lady of the *ton* on her doorstep, was flabbergasted to find her former charge there, dressed as a male. She quickly recovered herself and saw to it that Lady Elinor was given opportunity to refresh herself.

Now she offered her unexpected guest a restorative cup of tea. Elinor apprised Miss Palmer of all that had taken place.

"I needed to get away quickly," she ended, "and I could think of nowhere else to go on such short notice that might not immediately occur to Uncle."

"Of course, dear," Miss Palmer soothed, "I am flattered that you thought of me. And of course you may stay here as long as need be."

"Thank you."

"Mrs. Garrison—my sister, you know—is visiting in the north so we may accommodate you easily. We have only the Hendersons to serve us, so it will not be the elegance you are accustomed to, but you are ever so welcome."

This little speech brought a lump to Elinor's throat. She knew the retired Miss Palmer and her widowed sister lived on very meager combined incomes and that an extra person was likely to pose a serious drain on their resources.

"I shall not impose on you overlong, I hope," Elinor said. "I spent the entire two days on that awful coach thinking about this situation. I have very little money—certainly not enough to sustain me until I can attain access to my inheritance at the age of five and twenty! So . . . it is imperative I find some way to make a living for myself."

"Oh, my dear, what can a woman of your station do to make her own way?" Genuine concern and worry shone in both her tone and her eyes as Miss Palmer patted her guest's hand.

"Exactly what you did once," Elinor said firmly. "I intend to find a position as a governess. I thought you might help me. I was a fairly apt pupil, was I not?"

"You were the best. But do you truly think you could carry it off, my dear? You have no idea how difficult that life can be in some households. Particularly for a young, pretty woman like you. I would not advise it. There must be some other way."

"I am open to suggestion, of course, but I have wracked my brain for an alternative. I cannot go to relatives. They would just turn me over to Uncle Brompton."

"What about your godmother? Surely she would help you."

"She is in Italy with the Princess of Wales and lord knows when she is likely to return to England. And quite honestly, I have no funds for such a trip. My brother's allowance is insufficient to satisfy his needs and mine, too. I can see no other way."

"But you will need references. . . . And there is still the matter of your appearance," Miss Palmer insisted.

"References can be forged. I shall pull my hair back into an unfashionable bun—or plait it. I can add some freckles to those I already have. I will certainly not dress as a lady of the *ton*. And look . . ." She reached for her reticule lying on a nearby chair and dug around in it. "I found these in a shop in one of the villages when the coach stopped."

She pulled out a pair of eyeglasses and put them on.

"Oh, my goodness," Miss Palmer said.

"People rarely see any more than they expect to see, you know," said Elinor. "They will expect to see a governess in my person and that is what they will see. It is not as though I shall be attending balls and routs with former schoolmates or would-be suitors."

"You do have a point there, my lady," Miss Palmer conceded. "But what about your name? And you would have to assume the demeanor of someone less than gentry, you know. You will not be allowed to go about voicing your own opinion and correcting your so-called betters—even when they are wrong. A governess is caught in limbo between being an ignorant servant and equal to her employers." There was a tinge of bitterness in her tone.

Elinor laughed. "Miss Palmer, you know me too well. But with your help, I think I can do this." Her tone became more serious. "Indeed, I must do it. I will not marry that repulsive old man!"

Since she could come up with no alternative herself, Miss Palmer finally acquiesced and entered fully into helping Elinor plan. She spent hours each day training the younger woman for a new way of life. The most serious obstacle—aside from curbing the fierce independence Lady Elinor had always exhibited—was obtaining the necessary documents, proof of proper training and adequate references. One day, as Miss Palmer entered the room that served as drawing room, morning room, and library for her and her sister, she was in a high state of excitement.

"See what I have found!" She thrust a sheaf of papers into Elinor's hand. "References. We need only alter the dates and you have genuine papers to show."

"But these are your own references," Elinor said, skimming through them. "Changing the dates would be simple enough, I think, but what about the name?"

"I see no reason why you cannot be Miss Harriet E. Palmer. After all, I am not going to seek another position at this time of my life. Nor am I likely to be moving in such circles as would recognize the name you use. And these papers are genuine—they have the seals used by my former employers and everything."

"It does seem the perfect solution," Elinor mused.

"It *is* perfect, my dear," Miss Palmer exulted. "None of them contains a direct reference to my age. The *E* could be *Elinor* as well as the *Elizabeth* my mother christened me."

"Yes, I can see that."

"My last employers, the Spensers, gave me a very good reference, indeed. What is more, I happen to know that they are on an extended visit to their son with the army in Belgium, though they were never wont to go into society much anyway. Any prospective employer would find it difficult to check your references too closely."

"Well, if you are sure you will not mind . . ." Elinor was dubious about using Miss Palmer's name, but could find no reasonable argument against it. *Except simple honesty,* she chastised herself. *But then,* any *assumed name is going to be dishonest, is it not?*

Adrian Whitson, Marquis of Trenville, sat at his desk with a satisfied smile on his face though there was no one else in the room to share his triumph. "There." He sealed a document. "That should put *finis* to the leaking of information to the wrong people in Paris and Vienna!"

A soft rap at the door interrupted this thought.

"Miss Palmer, my lord."

"Ah, yes. The governess." Adrian came from behind his desk, bowed perfunctorily over the hand of the young woman shown into his library, and motioned her to a chair near the unlit fireplace.

"Please inform her grace that Miss Palmer is here," he said to the butler and took a seat opposite her. "My work in the Foreign Office keeps me away from home a good deal of the time and my mother has often been with the children. Since she has had more experience at this sort of thing than I, with your permission, I should like her to join us for this interview, Miss Palmer."

"Of course," she said politely.

He looked at the woman carefully. He had noted her to be of medium height, perhaps a bit shorter. She carried herself well. She had light brown hair, parted in the middle and pulled back into a bun on the nape of her neck; a straight, well-shaped nose; and a firm jaw and chin. Would she be inclined to be stubborn? he wondered. A generous sprinkling of freckles splashed across her nose. Ah, perhaps she will not be averse to spending time out-of-doors with the children. His perusal came to an abrupt halt with her eyes. Behind a pair of ordinary eyeglasses were the most extraordinary eyes he had ever seen. An intriguing shade of gray-green—like certain pieces of Oriental jade, he thought. Nor did the spectacles camouflage delicately arched dark brows and dark lashes. She smiled nervously, drawing his attention to her mouth. Too wide for conventional beauty, he mused, then abruptly brought himself to the task at hand.

"I beg your pardon," he said. "I did not mean to stare."

She nodded, acknowledging his statement, and withdrew some papers from a packet she carried. "My references, your lordship," she said, handing them to him.

"References. Yes, of course."

There were a few moments of silence as he looked them over. His eyebrows rose significantly and he was about to say something when the door opened and his mother swept into the room. Both he and Miss Palmer rose at her entrance.

"Miss Harriet Palmer, my mother, Duchess of Wallenford."

"Your grace." Miss Palmer curtsied to the other woman and turned to the marquis. "My lord, I am accustomed to using my second name which is *Elinor.*"

"All right. Miss *Elinor* Palmer is here about the governess position," Adrian said unnecessarily.

"Yes, I assumed as much," the duchess said, taking a seat and waving them back to theirs. She subjected the younger woman to the same scrutiny her son had. "You seem rather young for a governess." She was blunt, but not unkind.

"I am nearly four and twenty, your grace—old enough to have been employed for some years." Miss Palmer looked at the duchess directly. There was a defensive note, but her voice was well-modulated, her accent upper class.

"Your references speak well for you," Adrian interjected in a matter-of-fact tone. He smiled politely, but his voice became faintly skeptical as he added, "Do you *really* speak all these languages?" He handed the papers to his mother.

"I speak French fluently," she said. "My German is adequate. My Spanish slightly less so. My Italian . . ." She shrugged slightly. "I am afraid my Italian is barcly social."

"Luckily, the children do not entertain many visitors from Italy," he said.

The duchess looked up. "You seem remarkably well educated for a female, Miss Palmer. You read Latin *and* Greek?"

Miss Palmer seemed to color up at the disbelieving tone. "Yes, Your Grace, I do," she said firmly. "My father was educated at Oxford and he thought daughters as worthy of schooling as sons."

"I see," the duchess murmured.

The marquis and his mother continued to query her about

her qualifications and her feelings about working with young children. She told them that, in addition to associations noted in her references, she had helped to rear her younger brother after her mother died. They informed her the position entailed caring for the marquis's twins, a boy and a girl, aged six. Their mother having died at their birth, the children had heretofore been largely in the care of nursery maids. It was past time to start their formal education. The governess would also have in her care his ward, the nine-year-old daughter of his late brother, the previous Marquis of Trenville.

All three children were presently residing in Devon. Since the marquis spent much of his time traveling for the Foreign Office, he preferred to keep them in his home seat, though they occasionally came to town with him. Would Miss Palmer object to removing to the country? No, Miss Palmer would not object at all.

Miss Palmer was then asked to wait across the hall for a few minutes as the marquis and his mother conferred.

"Well?" He raised a quizzical brow.

"She is very impressive," his mother said slowly.

"But you have doubts."

"Not about her education and she strikes me as someone who can handle children . . ."

"But . . . ?" His tone was impatient.

"I do not think she is telling us all there is to know of one Miss Palmer."

"Good lord, Mother. Even a governess is entitled to her privacy. What did you see that I did not?"

"It is probably nothing. Just that the cut and quality of her clothing—not to mention its current style—is superior to what one expects of a governess."

"Seemed perfectly ordinary to me."

"I am sure it did." Her tone was dry. "Still," she added, "it is not unusual for a governess to receive an employer's cast-off clothing."

"Miss Palmer does not seem the type for castoffs," Adrian said.

"Whatever type that is," his mother replied. "Well . . . she seems decidedly superior to others we have interviewed. And we have talked with how many—five? Six? I would not have allowed that last one near my grandchildren. I suggest you hire Miss Palmer for a trial period at least."

Miss Palmer—the real Miss Palmer—had been waiting anxiously for Elinor to return.

"You certainly came home in style," she said, as Henderson stood by to take Elinor's pelisse and bonnet. "How did the interview go?"

Elinor whirled before her. "You see before you Miss Harriet Elinor Palmer, governess to the children and ward of the Marquis of Trenville. He insisted on sending me home in a carriage."

"My goodness. A position on your very first application! When are you to start? I hope you held out for a decent salary."

"I did not have to. What they offered was most generous. I think they were impressed that I can do more than read and write and embroider." Elinor laughed and grabbed Miss Palmer about the waist to dance a step or two. "Oh, thank you, thank you for helping me. I am finally truly confident this will work."

"Of course it will, my dear," said Miss Palmer, infected by Elinor's enthusiasm. "We must celebrate. Henderson, some sherry, please. Now, tell me." She ushered Elinor into the drawing room.

Elinor quickly summarized the events of the early afternoon.

"And," she ended, "I am to report for duty tomorrow. I am to stay at the Trenville town house tomorrow and the next morning we will depart for Devon, for that is where the children are."

"So soon?" Miss Palmer asked with regret. "I have so enjoyed having you here. And I shall miss you."

"And I, you," Elinor said. "But the sooner I am out of the city, the better, I am sure." *And,* she thought, *I will no longer be a drain on your resources, dear friend.*

That night she lay in bed recalling the interview. Working for the marquis would be a challenge. He had been polite and gracious, albeit reserved and proud—not unusual in a man of his status, she told herself. *And what does it matter, so long as he is satisfied with the performance of your duties? All that matters is that you stay hidden for the next twelve months.* But her thoughts strayed back to the person of her employer.

He was tall and sturdy-looking. He had deep brown hair and eyes, a broad forehead, well-defined brows, and high cheekbones. His nose might have been straight once, but it now had a slight bump in it as though it had been broken at some time. Rather an ordinary-looking man, she thought, until he smiled with a flash of brilliant white teeth and a shallow dimple that appeared only on the left side. The laugh crinkles at his eyes belied his rather austere demeanor. *I'll wager that smile has captured many a heart at a London ball,* Elinor mused.

Under ordinary circumstances, their social paths might have crossed before now, but after her obligatory season in Town, she had spent but little time in the city. She knew Trenville had come into his title when his older brother died of a fever. The current marquis had married the reigning debutante three years before Elinor had made her own come-out. Lady Beatrice had died in childbirth and rumor had it that the marquis was in no hurry to marry again. He was, of course, considered a prime catch by many an aspiring miss and her matchmaking mama.

The interview had gone well, she thought. Both the marquis and his mother seemed to have accepted Elinor's—that is, Miss Palmer's—credentials at face value. She had tried to answer all their questions with the truth as it applied to herself whenever possible. The fewer lies to keep in mind, the better. Still, she was not at all sure that the duchess did not harbor suspicions. She would have to be careful on that coach journey with the older woman.

Two

The next day Trenville's coachman was prompt in calling for Elinor. As her meager belongings were stowed on the carriage, she bid Miss Palmer and the Hendersons good-bye. She had posted a letter to her brother, telling him only that she had taken a position she was certain would provide for her adequately and instructing him again not to worry.

She still feared her uncle's finding her and dragging her back to marry the repulsive baron. She had awakened from horrifying dreams twice in the last week. She managed to quell these feelings, though, and she was rather looking forward to this new adventure in her life. There was something exciting about actually being another person for a while—and, after all, she would return to her own self and her own life soon enough.

On arrival at the Trenville town house, Elinor was shown to a well-appointed room near the now idle schoolroom and other rooms set aside for children. The marquis and his mother were out, but they had instructed that a tray be delivered to her room for tea and she was to join them later for dinner. Elinor freshened up and readied herself for dinner.

Dinner was rather informal as there were only the marquis, his mother, his secretary, a Mr. Huntington, and herself. Thomas Huntington was some five or six years younger than his employer—mid-twenties, Elinor thought.

He had reddish blond hair and blue eyes. He displayed a ready smile and there was a clean and wholesome look about him. In some undefinable way, he made her think of Peter.

"I understand you will be journeying to Devon on the morrow, Miss Palmer," he said conversationally as they were introduced in the drawing room before dinner.

"Yes," she replied. "I am quite looking forward to it, for I have never been there, nor have I lived near the sea."

"Where do you hail from, my dear?" the duchess asked.

"I beg your pardon?" Elinor asked to gain time to think. Had any of Miss Palmer's papers mentioned a place of origin?

"Where is your home?" the duchess repeated.

"Yorkshire, Your Grace." She settled on an area near her own native Lincolnshire and mentally crossed her fingers that there was nothing to the contrary in those papers. "But not at all near the sea."

"The seaside can be quite glorious when the weather co-operates," Huntington said.

"I quite like the sea even in a storm," Trenville offered.

"Comes from your years as a sailor, I daresay." Huntington turned to Elinor to add, "Trenville was with Nelson in the Mediterranean, you know."

"No. I did not know. How very interesting." First the navy, now the Foreign Office, she thought. Was he motivated by desire to serve, or by desire for power? She looked at him speculatively. He inclined his head in the slightest of not-quite-embarrassed bows and smiled at her. She felt a bolt of warmth jolt through her and quickly lowered her gaze.

"Adrian loved the sea in all its moods even as a small boy," the duchess said. "I must admit there is something awe-inspiring in the fierce uncontrolled power of a storm on the sea coast. But these days, I much prefer Wallenford's seat in Wiltshire."

"Only because Father rarely leaves the place," Trenville teased.

"I think he has you there, Your Grace." Huntington grinned at her.

"Well . . ." The older woman pretended hauteur.

Just then dinner was announced. With only the four of them in attendance, the conversation continued for the rest of the evening in a generally light vein. The others were careful to enlighten Miss Palmer on people and places they mentioned. She learned that the marquis's home in Devon was called Whitsun Abbey and had actually been part of a monastery until Henry VIII had awarded the property to an ancestor of the current residents for services not fully delineated for succeeding generations.

"That worthy ancestor also appropriated the name of the abbey for a family name," the duchess said, "though he changed the spelling—out of ignorance or a fit of anti-clerical sentiment. Who knows?" She chuckled.

Miss Palmer also learned the household included, in addition to the children already mentioned, his lordship's widowed sister-in-law, the dowager Marchioness of Trenville, as well as her companion.

The next morning, Adrian observed that it was quite an entourage setting out for Devon. He himself would alternately ride his mount and join the ladies in the Wallenford carriage. Another, less elegant carriage transported luggage, the marquis's valet, his French chef, and the duchess's personal maid. Miss Palmer was invited to join the duchess in her finely appointed traveling coach embossed with the crest of the Duke of Wallenford. The secretary was to await certain dispatches in London before following them in a few days.

Adrian appreciated efficiency in the people who worked for him. He hoped the new governess would fit that mold.

God knew this business of finding someone merely to teach young children had taken far more time and attention than he had anticipated. So far, he found little to criticize in this latest addition to his household. Her conversation the night before had been lively and knowledgeable, her questions intelligent and showing genuine interest. He suspected she may have held back on offering an opinion a time or two, but such behavior was understandable in light of her position and on such short acquaintance. At least she was not the shy, retiring mouse of a woman usually associated with that role.

He found himself considering the more personal attributes of his new employee. Since his mother's comment about her clothing, Adrian had paid more attention than was his wont. She did wear her garments well—and she had an enticing figure on which to hang them, he thought. She would probably make quite a splash in a fashionable ball gown. And a man could drown in those eyes.

Enough, he told himself. Whitson men do not take advantage of females in their employ. It makes absolutely no difference what she looks like so long as she handles her schoolroom duties adequately. However, his pompous self-flagellation did not prevent his mind from wandering back to her frequently in the course of the journey. He was tempted to simply enjoy her company in the coach and as he shared meals with the ladies After all, there no sin in a man's appreciating an attractive woman, no matter who she was.

On the other hand, this was no time to lose control of the rigid self-discipline he had practiced for more than six years now.

By the end of the long, tiring journey, both Elinor and the duchess drooped with exhaustion. When the carriage finally entered the long driveway of Whitsun Abbey, Elinor observed the duchess's demeanor brighten considerably.

"Thank goodness we have had good weather for these days of travel." The duchess enthusiastically leaned forward to glance out the coach window. "Just look at the sea in the distance. I do love this place."

"It is quite lovely," Elinor said, trying to take it all in at once. "The Abbey looks as though it were born to this spot." It was constructed of large gray stones overgrown with ivy that, at this time of the year, displayed a myriad of colors—varying shades of green, gold, vermilion, and brown. With the sea in the distance, it was a sight to behold. But it was not only the Abbey that was a sight to behold, she thought, as its owner came into view.

What was it about this man that caused such heightening of her senses? She could not recall ever having met another man whose mere personal presence caused her to react so. *Stop being such a ninny,* she scolded herself. *He is your employer. You are the governess, not some simpering schoolroom miss.*

The duchess interrupted her thoughts. "I first came here as a bride. This property has always been one of my favorites."

"I can readily see why," Elinor murmured politely.

"Adrian was born here and grew up here—that is, until he went away to school. Now that I think on it, neither of my sons truly lived at the Wiltshire seat, except for school holidays. Adrian prefers this place above all other Trenville and Wallenford holdings." The duchess babbled on in her delight at returning to the Abbey. "My husband, though, grew up in Wiltshire and much prefers it, though we were quite happy here until he inherited the Wallenford title. Oh, it has been an age since I was here—and I do love it best in autumn."

As the carriage came to a stop, Elinor smiled at her companion's pleasure. The duchess had maintained a polite formality throughout the journey, confining herself to general topics. Now she seemed almost garrulous—and as excited as a schoolgirl. The marquis was there promptly to hand his mother down, then turned to her fellow traveler. As she had been at all their stops along the way, Elinor was instantly aware of his physical presence when he took her hand to help her alight.

"Welcome to Whitsun Abbey, Miss Palmer," he said. "I hope you will enjoy Devon."

"I am sure I shall." She breathed deeply of the salt air and tried to maintain her composure. "It is very beautiful here," she added, looking off to where the late afternoon sun sparkled on the water.

"You are seeing it at its best," he affirmed. "September is always the loveliest time to visit the seaside."

In the entrance hall, Miss Palmer was introduced to Riverton, the butler. His greeting to the new governess was all that was rigidly proper, in sharp contrast to the controlled warmth he had shown the duchess on welcoming her back to what had once been her home. Elinor was shown to her room as the marquis and his mother proceeded directly to the schoolroom to greet the children. Miss Palmer was asked to join them a bit later.

She removed her bonnet and pelisse and surveyed her surroundings. This chamber was as comfortable and inviting as the one in London. She wondered if Trenville took care of all his employees this well and decided he probably did. She freshened up and reported to the schoolroom.

There she found the duchess had already gone to her own chamber to rest before dinner, but the marquis was still there, hugging a child on each knee, and listening with interest to a story from the third child whom Elinor assumed to be his niece. She was struck by the utter domesticity of the scene.

Here was a new view of her reserved employer. So far she had seen him as an aristocrat, one who took seriously the duties of his positions in society and the government. Here was a father who clearly enjoyed his children. Her own father had been such a man. So, why, Papa, did you give someone like Uncle Brompton such control over Peter and me? Then she upbraided herself. *Do stop wallowing in self-pity!* She smiled at the family grouped before her.

"Ah, Miss Palmer. May I introduce my children? This is my daughter, Lady Elizabeth, and my son Geoffrey, Viscount Templeton." At his urging the children climbed down from his lap and executed a very proper curtsy and bow.

"How nice to meet you, my lady, your lordship." She addressed the children and formally curtsied back to them. The little girl giggled.

"And this young lady is my niece, Lady Anne." The older girl curtsied correctly.

"Your ladyship." Elinor greeted her as formally as she had the others.

The three children eyed her inquisitively.

"Miss Palmer is your new governess," Trenville explained. "You must be very nice to her and do exactly as she bids you."

The two younger children nodded solemnly, but stayed close to their father. The older girl, a beautiful child with blond hair so light it was almost white, gave her a tentative smile, but her eyes, which were an intense deep blue, showed cautious reserve.

"Will you teach me to read?" Geoffrey asked shyly. "I already know my letters."

"So do I," Elizabeth interjected. "I want to read, too."

"Of course you do, my lady," Elinor said, then addressed both of them, "and we shall certainly learn to read."

"I already know how to read," Anne said importantly. "Mama says I shall soon have no need of a governess."

"I can see that you are quite a grown-up young miss, my lady. We shall try to build upon what you already know," Elinor replied.

"Miss Palmer," the marquis said as he stood, "you may dispense with the children's titles until they truly are quite grown. This is Bess, Geoffrey, and Anne." He patted each on the head.

"As you please, my lord."

"The children will take dinner here with the nursery maid, Miss Palmer, but my mother and I shall expect you to join us."

"Thank you, my lord."

He named the hour and then left the room, leaving her to get acquainted with her charges. A wave of sheer panic washed over her. What did *she* know of teaching? Or, indeed, of young children? True, she had always been close to her younger brother, but Peter had not been as young as these children for several years.

The four of them stared at each other for a moment. Then the twins both spoke excitedly.

"There are puppies in the stable," Geoffrey said.

"And kittens!" Bess added.

"Perhaps you will show them to me tomorrow," Elinor suggested.

"Uncle said I am to have a pony soon." Anne was obvious in her desire to be included.

"How exciting," Elinor said. "I had a pony when I was your age. I loved him dearly. His name was Ali Baba and we had great fun together."

"You did?" The little girl clearly disbelieved her. "Mama said a governess would not know anything of riding."

Instantly aware that her nervousness had allowed her to reveal more than she should have, Elinor responded thoughtfully to this challenge. "I daresay she is right about most governesses. Few are familiar with such sport. But I am."

"Oh."

For the next half hour the children vied with each other to entertain the new governess and introduce her to their favorite toys. Then it was time for their evening meal and for Miss Palmer to prepare herself for dinner.

As she changed into a simply designed gray gown of very light wool, she thought longingly of the ivory silk hanging in the armoire of her chamber in Lincolnshire. White lace at the wrists and a lace fichu were the only relief to the severity of the gray dress. Fastening a gold locket, she started for the door, then remembered her glasses.

"Best not forget these," she told herself. "Something to hide behind."

The butler showed her into the drawing room already occupied by the duchess and one of the most stunningly beautiful women Elinor had ever beheld. She was blond with striking blue eyes. Just like her daughter's, Elinor thought, for this woman had to be Anne's mother. Another woman of indeterminable age and modest dress accompanied them.

"Ah, come in, my dear," the duchess said. "Allow me to introduce my daughter-in-law, the Marchioness of Trenville. And Madame Giroux, her companion. Gabrielle, this is Miss Palmer."

"Your ladyship. Madame." Elinor curtsied very slightly.

"Miss Palmer." The marchioness nodded her greeting. Elinor noticed that the beauty spoke with a marked accent. The companion said nothing, but did acknowledge the newcomer by inclining her head. Madame Giroux was a small mouse of a woman with bright, beady eyes that missed very little.

"Gabrielle and her companion are French," the duchess said. "Lady Trenville's family fled the Terror when she was very young. Madame Giroux joined her a few years ago."

"Maria remains very French, but I am thoroughly English now, I fear." Gabrielle had a silvery laugh.

"Not too thoroughly English," Adrian said, entering the room. "Hello, Gabbi." He greeted his sister-in-law in the French fashion, kissing her on each cheek. "Ladies," he directed to his mother, Madame Giroux, and Miss Palmer.

Elinor watched with interest as the marchioness seemed to blossom at his attention. The woman was, indeed, a charmer. Fair of face and figure, she was in her early thirties, Elinor conjectured. Without her seeming in any way to command such, the conversation throughout the evening centered on topics of interest to the French woman. She wanted to know all the latest *on dits* from Town and shared similar gossip of the local area.

Adrian met with his steward the next day and the two of them conducted an inspection tour of the rather vast acreage that constituted his main holding, Whitsun Abbey. As they rode along, Jenkins apprised his lordship of local events of interest.

"Are our nocturnal workers still engaged in their trade?" Adrian asked with exaggerated irony.

"I am afraid so, my lord." Jenkins shook his head. "Not as much as before the war ended, but as you well know, there are still many who would rather buy and sell their cognac without customs men being involved. And our beaches *are* convenient."

"Yes. I am sure that many a bottle in my own cellars came into the country that way," Adrian admitted ruefully.

"There seem to be only two local gangs operating now. They respect each other's territory and customers. Stay out of each other's hair, don't you know?"

"We know who they are?"

"Oh, yes. The militia hauls a few of them before the magistrate once in a while. A couple of them—really brutal fellows they were—have been transported."

"I suppose we should crack down harder on the whole lot." Adrian knew that, as he was the area's principal landowner, it was up to him to initiate such a move. "I hate to do that in these hard times. There are already far too many men roaming the highways out of work."

"The way it is, it is easier to keep an eye on the business," Jenkins offered.

"There is that."

"Drive them underground and there's no telling who's doing what."

"So, who *is* doing what?" Adrian asked.

"Total of ten, fifteen, maybe more. It varies with the particular job or shipment. Fred Jones from over at Bimford heads one of the gangs."

"Jones?" Adrian did not recognize the name.

"His folks own an inn in Bimford—Three Sails West it's called."

"Oh, yes. And the other?"

The steward glanced obliquely at his employer, cleared his throat, and spoke quietly. " 'Tis your housekeeper's son, my lord."

"Little Bobby Hoskins? You cannot be serious."

Jenkins laughed. "He's not so little these days, sir. Big strapping lad, he is, with a wife and babe of his own."

"All the more reason for him not to be involved in such shady dealings then."

"Right, my lord. But if you were to acknowledge you knew about the smuggling, you'd have to take formal action, wouldn't you?"

"Probably. But a word to his mother should suffice as a warning."

Three

As she climbed into bed the next night, Elinor assured herself the first day had gone well. There had been few actual lessons, but she had become better acquainted with the children—and their beloved puppies and kittens. On their way to the stables, little Bess had shyly placed her small hand in Elinor's. The gesture signaled the little girl's acceptance and Elinor was strangely warmed by it. Later in the day, Geoffrey, too, had come around, bringing a special offering, a flutterby he had captured in his cupped hands. Anne was less ready to extend a wholehearted welcome to this new adult in their lives and frequently offered authoritative advice and warnings in a tone obviously borrowed from some adult.

"Children are not allowed in the stables or outbuildings. . . . Bess, mind you do not get grass stains on your skirt. . . . Keep to the paths now. . . . Geoff, do stop racing around like a chicken."

Elinor tried, without much success, to distract Anne from her officious and domineering attitude. *Perhaps she does not receive sufficient attention,* Elinor mused, though Anne's uncle had accorded her extraordinary attention the day before and the promised pony did not indicate neglect on his part. However, the child's mother had not made an appearance with the schoolroom set. Perhaps Anne needed to feel important—and loved. Something to work on.

The following day a pattern was established for the activities of the new governess and her charges. Elinor rose early each morning and took a walk around the grounds before breakfast. Sometimes she then had the sunny family breakfast room all to herself, for the other ladies were not early risers. Occasionally, the marquis was there before her. After an exchange of polite greetings, he would ask penetrating questions about the children's lessons, even suggesting works from his own library that might be helpful, at least to their teacher. Meanwhile, servants assigned to the care of the children would ready them for the morning's lessons.

Spending her days with her charges, Elinor welcomed the chance for adult company in the evenings. Although she invariably had fleeting regrets about her limited wardrobe as she changed for dinner, she spent little time lamenting the loss of pretty clothes.

One evening as she entered the drawing room prior to the announcement of dinner, Elinor was pleased to see that Thomas Huntington had joined the group.

"I am surprised to see you so soon, Mr. Huntington. I understood you would be in London at least a week after we left," she commented after greeting him and the others.

"Actually, it was nearly a week, but I made the journey in less time than you. Of course, I had the advantage of traveling lightly. And alone." He smiled.

"You must indeed have made good time then."

"Sealed dispatches from the Foreign Office require the utmost expediency," he said, adopting a teasingly pompous tone.

"Oh, I see." She smiled at him.

"Sherry, Miss Palmer?" The marquis offered her a glass.

"Thank you," she said, briefly looking into his eyes, recognizing the now familiar tingle as their hands touched when he gave her the glass. She quickly lowered her gaze.

Both men were dressed casually, but elegantly. However,

Elinor noted to herself, Adrian commanded one's attention more intensely. She pulled herself up short. Just when did the Marquis of Trenville become "Adrian" to her? She turned to engage the ladies in conversation until dinner was soon announced.

In the drawing room later, Gabrielle entertained them with a practiced, if less than stirring performance on the pianoforte. Both the duchess and Madame Giroux were occupied with needlework as Elinor idly leafed through a copy of *La Belle Assemblee*. Huntington and the marquis seemed content just to listen. Then tea was served and the footman bearing it left the room as the duchess began to pour.

"Come, Thomas." Gabrielle patted the seat next to her as she moved to the settee, pronouncing his name in her enchanting Gallic accent. "You must share with us the latest *on dits* from Town."

Elinor put aside her magazine to take the cup the Duchess offered. She glanced at Adrian. He seemed amused at his sister-in-law's undisguised delight in gossip.

Huntington laughed and took the seat she indicated. "I doubt I have much to offer beyond what the others have already told you," he said with a nod in the direction of their companions.

"Surely there is something," she wheedled.

"Hmm. Well, yes, I think there is. Seems Melbourne's wife has become quite *outre* in her pursuit of the poet, Byron."

"No! Tell me!" She clasped her hands before her.

"Yes," he assured her, accepting the cup the duchess handed him. "Dressed herself as a page to gain admittance to a rout he was attending. Stirred quite a furor, I'm told."

"And how did his lordship react to that?" asked the duchess.

"Which one—Melbourne or Byron?" Huntington responded.

"Both." Her grace chuckled.

"Melbourne whisked his wife off to the country forth-with and Byron seems to be avoiding company—at least until the gossip dies down."

"Oh, how rich." Gabrielle laughed. "What else?"

"Seems an heiress has disappeared," Huntington said, warming to his task.

Intuitively, Elinor froze, her cup halfway to her mouth. She slowly lowered it, taking care it did not rattle against the saucer. She gripped the saucer tightly.

"Who?" Gabrielle's voice was a delighted little squeal.

"No one we know," Huntington said. "Sister to the new Earl of Ostwick, but he is still a schoolboy. They are trying to keep it close as wax, but the guardian was in Town making inquiries."

"Is foul play suspected?" the marquis asked.

"Apparently not." Huntington shrugged. "The lady seems to have run away on her own."

"With a lover?" Gabrielle asked.

"Trust a Frenchwoman to read romantic intrigue into it," Huntington said, laughing. "Who knows? There was some vague talk of a match, but I forget with whom."

"Perhaps she disliked the match and ran away with a lover of her own choice," Gabrielle said.

Elinor tried to look relaxed, though she sat rigidly, unable to look at any of them lest her eyes give her away. Panic gripped her as the marchioness guessed at least half the truth.

"Ostwick," the duchess mused. "I believe the family name is Richards. What is the lady's name then?"

"I did not catch it truly," Huntington said with another shrug. "Helen—or Ellen. Something like that. Melanie, maybe."

"Well," the duchess said dismissively, "let us hope she has not been compromised in any way. Caroline Lamb's antics seem far more serious. Melbourne is an ambitious man."

Elinor breathed a soft inward sigh of relief as the conversation veered away from the runaway heiress. She set her tea aside and began leafing through the magazine again, but took little note of what she saw.

Presently the marquis's deep voice caught her attention as he addressed Huntington.

"You are certainly as familiar with this area as I am, Tom. Would you say the smuggling trade has become more marked recently?"

"Mr. Huntington's father was steward here when my husband was marquis," the duchess said to Elinor. "Thomas ran freely with my children as they were growing up. His mother still lives in the village."

"I would not say it is any worse," Huntington said slowly. "Probably about the same, despite the end of hostilities with the French. Chance for locals to pick up some extra coin occasionally. Why do you ask?"

"Just wondering if I should do something about it," Adrian said.

"Certain it is that you have the authority to do so," Huntington responded. "However, I should think it would be easier to keep track of the trade if you did not require them to sneak around any more than they already do."

Adrian nodded. "That is exactly what Jenkins said."

"But surely, you cannot condone such activity, my son," the duchess admonished.

"I am not condoning it, Mother. Merely not making a larger issue of it than need be."

"Well . . ." She sounded dubious.

"And to that end," he went on, "before you return to Wallenford on the morrow, I should like you to have a friendly word with Mrs. Hoskins about her son's evening activities. It would be better coming from another woman, I think."

"Little Bobby Hoskins?" The duchess was aghast.

Adrian gave a bark of laughter. "That was my reaction, too. Little Bobby Hoskins," he affirmed. "Now, if you all will excuse me, I must look at those dispatches Thomas brought with him."

Sometimes Elinor took the midday meal below with the other adults; sometimes she joined the children. Then, the twins would be put down for naps—not without protest—and Elinor would accompany Anne to the music room to give the girl a lesson on the pianoforte. Anne, of course, had not the training and practice her mother showed, but she had genuine feeling for her music. Anne still treated the new governess with less warmth than the others did, though she had shed a few of her reservations. She was cooperative and actually welcomed the music lessons.

Knowing full well that most men of the *ton* spent as little time with their offspring as possible, Elinor was surprised at the interest shown by the marquis. Indeed, he seemed to guard his regularly scheduled time with his children almost jealously. In the afternoon, when their lessons were finished, he would take the twins out in the gig, driving into the village or about the estate, or perhaps he would take them for a stroll in the gardens.

Sometimes Anne accompanied them, but often this was the time she spent with her mother in that lady's chambers or in the drawing room. Elinor had learned early on that the presence of the marchioness at the Abbey was rather a "seasonal" event. The beautiful Frenchwoman preferred Town life, though she usually left her daughter at the Abbey "so as not to cause instability in a child's life." Elinor was of the opinion that her concern for stability conveniently allowed the marchioness to ignore some of her responsibilities to her daughter. A few idle comments in conversations between the duchess and her daughter-in-law suggested that Gabrielle had been extremely disappointed when she produced a mere girl, instead of the next Marquis of Trenville and eventual heir to a dukedom.

In any event, Elinor thought, Anne must sense her mother's latent disappointment and indifference. Elinor's heart went out to this child who was the same age she had been when she lost her mother. How much worse it must be for Anne whose mother was still a presence in her life, but just did not seem to care.

There was only so much a governess could do about this situation, but Elinor resolved to do all in her power to see that Anne was not unduly hurt—at least so long as the child was in her care. Knowing what solace it could offer, she encouraged Anne's interest in music. She also made a point of praising the girl, both to build Anne's confidence and to acquaint others, especially the child's mother, with how worthy she was.

Several days had passed with little substantive communication between the governess and her employer. Then, one morning at breakfast, he required an accounting.

"I trust all goes well with the schoolroom set," he said, laying aside his reading as she took a seat.

"Quite well, my lord. We are plotting a course to sail around the world."

"Bess and Geoffrey seem a bit young for advanced levels of geography."

"I agree. But they are responding well to questions about how children might live in other parts of the world."

"I see . . ." he said, his voice indicating he did not see at all.

"You know: how other children dress, the games they play, how they live. We can touch on different cultures without too much business of latitude and longitude or prevailing wind patterns."

"I see." And this time he did. "Sounds appropriate."

"We are having great fun—and, I hope, learning in the process. Anne is a help; she is quite eager in researching various locations."

"You seem to get on well with the three of them."

"I think so. Bess and Geoffrey are at that eager-to-please stage when the teacher is always a genius."

"And Anne?"

"Anne is more cautious," she said hesitantly. "She seems to be waiting—"

"Waiting? For what?"

"I think to see if she should invest her trust."

"Anne had a difficult time with her last governess. We thought it best that you form your own impression before saying anything of previous problems."

"She does not hold a very high opinion of governesses in general," Elinor said with a laugh. "But we are working through that."

"How?"

"She loves music. I think it is helping her cope with her feelings and anxieties."

"The last governess described her as bossy, rebellious, and sulky," Adrian said bluntly.

"She does like to be the one in charge, but I really think . . ." Her voice trailed off as—too late—she thought better of sharing her view of the situation. She recalled Harriet Palmer's warning to her.

"Yes? You really think . . . come on, Miss Palmer—out with it," he commanded.

"I think Anne desperately needs to feel wanted, needed," she said in a rush.

"I am not sure I know what you mean." His voice had gone decidedly cool. "She is certainly not neglected. She is included in everything involving my own children."

"Sometimes a child's perception of herself or a situation has little to do with reality. It seems to me that Anne's tendency to direct and control stems from feelings of inadequacy." Oh, lord. Now she had done it. Why had she not just left the lid on this particular container?

He was quiet for several minutes, apparently mulling over what she had said.

"Hmm. Do you have a remedy then?"

"Well, not precisely a remedy. But I do have suggestions."

"Somehow I thought you might," he said, the ease back in his voice and a twinkle in his eyes.

"I believe she needs to have her self-confidence bolstered whenever the opportunity presents itself."

"And . . ."

"And perhaps something that is hers alone to care for. A pet perhaps? One of the first things Anne ever said to me was that Uncle Adrian was going to allow her to have a pony."

"Yes. I did promise her that. You truly believe it will help?"

"At the very least, it could do no harm."

"I will look into it."

Adrian set himself to enjoying the few weeks he would have at Whitsun Abbey before government business again dragged him off to London or the Continent. Meanwhile, a courier arrived every few days with dispatches. After each arrival, Adrian retreated to his library for a considerable time to decode and respond to the messages. When the marquis emerged, the courier would be sent on his way again. Occasionally, Thomas Huntington was asked to join him in drafting some document.

One day as the two were working individually in the library, Adrian at his desk, Huntington at a large library table, Adrian seemed to be struggling with a particular message.

"Anything I can help you with?" Huntington asked.

"Eh? . . . er . . . no." Adrian seemed to have forgotten he was not alone. "No, thanks. This must be encoded and I am just having a bit of trouble trying to phrase it so that neither the Russians nor the Austrians will misunderstand when it is decoded in Vienna."

"Teach me the code and I'll do it for you," Huntington

joked, for both knew the code was known to only seven persons in the government—and two of those were negotiating in Vienna.

"Would that I could! You are often better at turning a phrase than I," Adrian responded.

"Are the reports we hear and read true regarding the Congress?" Huntington asked, his tone conversational.

"I'm afraid so. The victorious allies are no nearer an agreement on disposition of Napoleon's empire than they were in April when he was banished to Elba. I would not hold much hope for a timely decision from the group gathering in Vienna."

"Nobody trusts anybody else, I take it?"

"You have the right of it," Adrian said. "That—and the French representative, Talleyrand, is turning out to be more clever than anyone expected."

"Vienna must be the gayest city on the continent these days." There was a wistful note in Huntington's voice.

"I am sure it is. Half of Europe's aristocrats have gathered there for parties and balls and routs. They feed like sharks on tidbits of gossip. Hard to tell where social intrigues end and political intrigues begin. I was damned glad to get away—even before the Congress convened." Adrian sanded the document and reached for the sealing wax.

"Will you be returning soon?"

"Perhaps . . . after the New Year. At least to Paris to confer with our ambassador there."

"Ah, yes. The inimitable Wellington."

There was a knock at the door and at Adrian's call to "Enter," Miss Palmer did little more than stick her head around the door.

"You asked me to tell you when the children were finished with lessons today, my lord," she said.

"Yes. We have planned an excursion into the village. Would you please inform Nurse to have them ready in, say, twenty minutes?" Adrian asked with a glance at a clock on the mantel.

"Certainly, my lord." Her head disappeared.

"Oh, Miss Palmer," he called. The head reemerged, the eyes questioning. "If you would care to accompany us, you would be most welcome."

"Thank you, my lord. I should like that very much."

When the door clicked shut, Adrian found Huntington looking at him with a pronounced grin on his face.

"Getting cozy with the new governess, are we?" the secretary teased.

"I would not think a trip to the village with three chattering youngsters would afford much in the way of 'coziness,'" Adrian replied, annoyed that he was bothering to explain. That was what came of employing fellows who had known one in short coats.

"You never know," Huntington said, wiggling his eyebrows lasciviously. "She's not a bad looker, that one."

"You forget yourself, Huntington. She is also in my employ and will be treated properly," Adrian said chillingly.

"Yes, my lord!" Huntington's knowing grin did not sit well with the marquis, but Adrian chose to ignore the other man's impudence.

Why *had* he asked her to come along?

Because, he answered himself, she has been here for over two weeks and has yet to leave the estate. Even a governess deserves an outing once in a while. And you will not mind in the least being in her company for a couple of hours, now will you? Exuberant children or no.

Goodness! Elinor told herself, had anyone suggested a few weeks ago she would be excited by the prospect of traipsing about a country village, she would have laughed them quiet. Now, here she was, happy as a frog in a bog, as Peter would say. The question was, was she so happy to have a change in her routine—or was it the idea of spending this time in the company of her employer?

She and Anne were seated in the landau across from the marquis and the twins. The children were, as children are wont to be, uninhibited and full of questions, observations, and not-so-subtle suggestions about what to see and do in the village. Occasionally, the marquis would glance at Miss Palmer to share adult amusement at the antics of the little people. Each time he caught her eyes, Elinor felt a ripple of pleasure sweep through her.

"Papa, may we see the shark? Please?" Geoffrey asked.

"Pooh! Who wants to see that old thing?" Anne objected. "I want to choose some pretty shells at Mr. George's shop."

"A shark?" Elinor inquired. "Surely not from these waters?"

"No." Adrian smiled. "Actually, Geoffrey refers to the skeletal remains of a shark that some ship's captain brought from the South Seas many years ago."

"Just some old fish bones." Anne gave a superior sniff.

"No. 'Tis truly a wonder, Miss Palmer," Geoffrey said seriously. "Please, Papa."

"If we are to show Miss Palmer all the sights of our village we shall certainly see the shark, Geoffrey. And, yes, Anne, you may choose some pretty shells. And what do you want to see, poppet?" He directed this last to Bess.

"Toffee." She giggled.

"I should have known. The sweet tooth in the family," her father noted.

The village was larger than Elinor had expected and cleaner than she remembered seacoast villages being when she had visited others with her father and brother. She commented on its size.

"West Benton *is* larger than most of its neighbors," Trenville agreed. "Local farmers trade here and the harbor accommodates small fishing boats nicely. Not to mention the occasional smuggler." He added the last in a rueful tone.

"The area does seem rich in resources for the table," Elinor said.

"Ah, here is our first stop—the fish market. Here you will find the venerable bones of one poor old shark." As he aided in her descent from the carriage and took her elbow to help her over the raised entrance, Elinor felt warmed where he touched her.

The fish market, a large barnlike building, was nearly overwhelming in its impact on the nose, Elinor thought. Inside were several large tables with raised edges at which men and women were working scaling, boning, and filleting fish of varying sizes and species.

Anne wrinkled her nose, but turned down the option of waiting at the door for the others.

"See! There it is!" Geoffrey exclaimed. "Isn't it just the most fearsome thing?"

Along one wall was displayed the full skeleton of a shark that must have been ten or twelve feet long when it plied the waters of some southern sea.

"Indeed it is," Miss Palmer agreed. "Those teeth look very sharp."

"Come ta see me shark again, have ye, me young lord?" An older man addressed Geoffrey. He was a strong-looking fellow with a splotchy white apron wrapped around considerable girth. His round face was clean-shaven except for a grizzled fringe running from ear to ear. His skin, too, looked grizzled—weathered by years of sun and wind. His blue eyes twinkled with welcoming delight. "Yer pa was just as fascinated with that thing as ye be when he were yer age."

"Don't you be telling all my secrets now, Jake," the marquis said with a sheepish smile. He introduced Miss Palmer to the fisherman.

"His lordship used to go out on me boat wi' us," the older man told her. "Yuh'd a made a right smart fisherman, my lord." Jake chortled at his own joke. "Mayhap this young feller would like to go out sometime."

"Oh, Papa, may I? Please? May I?"

"We will see," his father said, adopting the tone of parents who, since the beginning of time, have been reluctant to commit themselves on the spot.

The children wandered around among the workers, clearly fascinated by the whole scene, especially when they witnessed the use of large, dangerous-looking knives. Elinor tagged along, keeping an eye to the safety of her charges and ever aware of the man at her side. She noted that Trenville addressed many of the workers by name and they seemed thoroughly at ease with him.

"May we see the fish ponds, Papa? They are just in the back," Geoffrey said.

"Shark's teeth are not enough, eh? Miss Palmer would you care to see the fish ponds?" Trenville gave her a look of mock conspiracy.

"Well . . . since we are here." She pretended reluctance and winked at Geoffrey who grinned back at her.

The ponds were set some distance from the main building. Elinor welcomed the relatively fresher air as they walked out to them.

"See how big these fishes are?" Geoffrey's excitement was hard to contain.

"What kind of fish are these, Geoffrey?" Elinor asked, knowing full well what they were, but wanting to give the little boy his moment of importance.

"In this pond are trout, and in that one over there are carp. Our village has both freshwater and ocean fish," he said. It seemed to Elinor that he probably echoed some grown-up. She smiled indulgently and again caught her employer's eye.

"Come, now," the marquis said. "Let us be about finding those shells and some toffee."

As the children skipped ahead, Trenville turned to her.

"Thank you," he said. When she looked at him inquiringly, he went on, "For allowing him to demonstrate his vastly superior knowledge."

"Of course," she murmured, pleased that he had noticed. "Geoffrey wanted to feel grown up."

In the end, each of the children was accorded a chance to feel important. Anne spent some time choosing just the right pretty shells for a necklace—or perhaps they were for a seashore picture—or perhaps she would just keep them in her treasure box. Then it was on to the bakery, which carried an enticing assortment of candies. By then, of course, Bess was not alone in seeking to satisfy a sweet tooth.

The wind picked up as the afternoon wore on, but there were a good many people about the street. Some had the look of purposeful intent signaling "important business" and others appeared to share the leisure of the marquis and his small ensemble, looking in windows, eyeing wares displayed outside doorways on tables, and stopping to share gossip now and then. Elinor drew her shawl more closely around her and thought nostalgically of her own village in Lincolnshire.

As the five of them returned to the carriage, several red-coated militia men trotted their horses down the street. Adrian swept his daughter into his arms and Elinor grabbed a hand of each of the others to hurry them out of the traffic. The militia men were nearly upon them when the leader of the group, sporting a captain's insignia, called out.

"Trenville? It *is* you." The captain halted his horse, dismounted, and offered Adrian his hand. "Nathan Olmstead. We met some weeks ago at Whitehall. This is a fortuitous meeting. I have orders to contact you."

Adrian looked at the man quizzically a moment, then took his hand and said, "Yes, of course. I recall the meeting."

"We are assigned to the barracks in Torquay." The captain

included the other riders in a gesture. "Since Bonaparte no longer poses a threat, the militia is charged with the task of trying to control smuggling."

"That is likely to prove a rather daunting task," Adrian observed dryly.

"Without a doubt. But we are to make a preliminary investigation of all the villages in this area, especially those with harbors and inlets—and to contact the principal land-owners to seek their cooperation."

"Perhaps you could come to the Abbey tomorrow to discuss this business," Adrian suggested. "I must return these children and their governess home now."

"I understand, my lord. Tomorrow, then."

As Adrian gave the captain directions to the Abbey, Elinor assisted the children into the carriage. The captain waved a farewell salute and they were off.

Four

The next day Captain Olmstead was shown into the library just as Adrian finished meeting with his steward. Olmstead was a tall man with black hair and gray eyes. He had even, pleasant features that narrowly missed being downright handsome. He held a packet in his hand as he took the seat offered.

"Well, Nate," the marquis said, "what was all that pretense about yesterday? What *are* you doing here, really? The War Office does not waste men of your talents on petty smugglers of the occasional barrel of brandy. Should you not be in Vienna sorting out cloak-and-dagger intrigues?"

Captain Olmstead laughed. "I was trying to establish for the men with me, and for any onlookers, that you and I are relative strangers. Don't want to compromise your credit with the locals, you know, by having them think you are so intimate with the chief excise man in the area."

"Why should that matter?" Adrian raised his eyebrows in surprise. "Chief excise man?"

"For the time being. Perhaps it does not matter at all. But I could not be sure, so I chose the way of caution. Take a look at this before we talk any farther."

Olmstead drew a document out of his packet and handed Adrian a memorandum marked "Urgent and Confidential."

"Why was this not sent with the regular courier?" Adrian

asked as he started to read. Then he turned startled eyes to his visitor. "I see why now. Damn!"

The captain nodded. "Just so. Somehow some very delicate information is still making its way to the French and our negotiators in Vienna are having a devil of a time. That wily Talleyrand always seems to know what he has no business knowing at all."

"The man is inordinately clever."

"It has become worse recently, for the sort of information he is obtaining now is more detailed and more accurate."

"I thought we nipped the problem with the arrest of Henri Pierre. That and changing the code on a frequent basis." Adrian's tone was impatient.

"Clever fellow, our Monsieur Pierre, was he not? Unobtrusive little fellow establishes himself as the lover of Lord Farrington's wife and *voila!* he has an excellent conduit for information from one pillow to another."

"Are we bringing charges against her?"

"No. Seems not. Canning and Castlereagh would like to do so, mind you. But to prosecute her would bring more information out in the open than anyone deems prudent. Farrington's career is ruined, of course. He has been advised to take his wife on an extended tour of Italy and then retire to the country."

"Perhaps that is just punishment for a woman who loved London society as much as she seemed to," Adrian said. "But, getting back to the current problem . . ."

"Yes. Well. Seems Monsieur Pierre was not alone in providing information to his countrymen. He was useful to them—devilishly so, in fact. But either we missed another source at the time, or they have managed to establish a new one in record time."

"I was so sure we had plugged that leak."

"We know that the information is not getting out of England by conventional means," Olmstead continued. "It almost has to be traveling from some small harbor on our coast, probably along avenues established by smugglers. Hence, my presence in your domain. In some cases, locals involved in the 'free trade' probably have no idea they are also dealing in espionage."

"Good grief! That makes looking for a needle in a hay-stack seem like child's play."

"True. But this particular spy appears to be someone close to one of the people presently in England with regular access to information being sent to our team in Vienna."

"Are you suggesting my courier or someone in my household is passing along information to the French?" Adrian asked flatly.

"Not necessarily. We have narrowed it down to *someone* close to you—or to Dennington, or Morton, or Canning—Castlereagh being out of the country."

"Narrowed it down?" Adrian's tone was rich with irony.

"You are right. That is overstating the case mightily. All of you have very large staffs spread over half of England. And two of you, you and Dennington, have major properties right on the coast."

Adrian sighed. "Dennington and I also both have close contacts with French émigrés. Dennington's wife is French. My sister-in-law still has relatives in Brittany. Her companion is French, too. So, where do we start in sorting this out? I assume you have something in mind or you would not be here in Devon."

"We start by looking at any new members of your staff. Have you hired new people in the last three or four months?"

"Yes. Several. The London housekeeper is fairly new—had to pension off her predecessor. Also, two of the footmen there as well as an upstairs maid. Perhaps others—the butler usually handles such hiring, you know. My coachman came to me in April. There is a groom in the stables who is new. And the children's governess came to us only a few weeks ago." Adrian was not sure why he hesitated slightly in mentioning the governess. "I can have a list drawn up."

"That would be helpful. As I said, we can start with new staff, but it could just as easily be someone that one of you has known for a long time. Who knows why a person would turn traitor? Greed? Fear? Blackmail?"

"It should be easy enough to rule out some of them. After all, it is highly unlikely this spy could be illiterate. Not many servants read and write."

"True. And while we are more apt to think of 'it' as a man, it could just as easily be a female. What about this new governess?"

"She came to us with excellent references. She is better educated than many a governess and she is exceptionally good with the children. Even my mother says she is a real find."

"She was with you yesterday?"

"Yes."

"Not bad looking, either."

For some reason this comment annoyed Adrian, but he remained silent.

Perhaps Nate's interest in Miss Palmer was not entirely professional. After all, some might consider them a suitable match. She seemed to come from impoverished gentry and, as the third son of a viscount, Nathan Olmstead could not be thought prime goods on the marriage mart—even if he *was* one of those people who move with ease in any social circle. Reasonable as this conjecture seemed, it did not sit well with his lordship, though he would have been at a loss to explain precisely why.

Olmstead had bought his commission soon after he and Trenville came down from Oxford and had quickly proved himself invaluable in gathering intelligence. The two men had seen little of each other in recent years, though their friendship went back to those school days. Their paths had crossed now and then if only via papers, for Adrian's office often acted upon intelligence gathered by Olmstead and others in the field.

The captain accepted Trenville's invitation to dinner, but turned down the suggestion that he stay at the Abbey. The pretense of their having only slight acquaintance might yet prove useful.

Having taken tea with the children, Elinor did not meet Captain Olmstead until she joined the family for dinner that evening. He was very pleasant to her and made every effort to be sure she, too, was included in the conversation. However, it was the beautiful Gabrielle who commanded most of his attention. This came as no surprise to Elinor. After all, she and Madame Giroux were the only other women present and neither of them could claim the degree of regard a member of a marquis's family could. In all honesty, Elinor admitted to herself, Gabrielle truly was charming as well as beautiful and tonight she seemed to be exerting herself to be all the more charming to a newcomer. It almost seemed an instinctive reaction for her, Elinor mused, unaware that the idea had brought a slight smile to her mouth.

"Are you going to share the fun, Miss Palmer?" the marquis asked.

She started. "I beg your pardon? Oh. I . . . I was just thinking of something the children said earlier. It was nothing. Really." She could not control the faint blush that crept upward.

He gave her an amused glance as much as to say "have it your way" and did not pursue the matter.

Gabrielle appropriated the captain's arm to take her in to dinner, leaving Adrian to escort the governess with Huntington and the companion close behind. Later, the women retired to the drawing room while the men finished their port and pursued such topics as occupied men at the end of a meal. The marchioness was all that was proper and polite in speaking with her companions, but she quite obviously was less than fully comfortable. She became increasingly impatient for the return of the gentlemen, glancing often at the door through which they would come. When the men did rejoin them, Gabrielle affected surprise that they were so prompt.

As the men took their seats, Huntington turned to the marchioness. "My lady, may we prevail upon you for some music this evening?" he asked.

"I should love to play for you dear gentlemen." She fairly simpered. "But my daughter tells me that Miss Palmer plays exceptionally well, and I think we should hear for ourselves."

Elinor was taken aback, for she had not played for the adults in this household. She glanced at the marquis who regarded her with an enigmatic expression. Did he think her out of her element with such a demand? And why was Gabrielle so willing to give up the opportunity to show off her feminine accomplishments? Did she think to show up an impertinent nobody with her own performance later?

"Well, then, Miss Palmer?" Huntington seemed a bit uncertain, but apparently saw no alternative.

"If it is the general wish, of course," she said, acceding to the situation. She rose and seated herself at the pianoforte.

"The music is under the seat, Miss Palmer," Gabrielle called.

"Thank you, my lady, but I think I shall not need it."

She saw Trenville's eyebrows rise at this. Huntington's concern that she would embarrass herself was writ plain on his face. Gabrielle exhibited one of her expressive little Gallic shrugs and exchanged a glance with Madame Giroux.

Elinor paused for a moment, thinking what to play. The instrument was placed at an angle in the room that allowed her to see her audience clearly. They waited expectantly.

"Ah. This one seems appropriate for the season," she

said and set her fingers to the keys. As soon as the first chords were struck, any sense of nervousness or apprehension left her and she gave herself up to the music.

Huntington looked at his companions questioningly.

Trenville nodded after a few bars and said, "Of course. Vivaldi's 'Autumn.' Good choice, Miss Palmer."

She was pleased to see him clearly settle himself to enjoying her presentation. Gabrielle chose to engage the captain in conversation, occasionally drawing Huntington's attention also. When she finished the piece, Trenville applauded enthusiastically and the others politely echoed his praise.

"Do give us another, Miss Palmer," Huntington said.

"Something lighter this time," Gabrielle suggested.

Feeling thoroughly at ease now, Elinor said, "All right. Here is a medley of some of my brother's favorites." She proceeded to play several popular Scottish airs, skillfully blending one tune into the next.

Gabrielle had rung for tea before Elinor finished playing, and now as the tray was brought in, Trenville rose to return the governess to her seat.

"Thank you, Miss Palmer. I had no idea we were graced with such talent in our midst. You must play for us again."

"By all means," Gabrielle said graciously. "I vow I shall be too embarrassed ever to play again." She gave a light laugh as though to show she was not serious in this "vow."

"I am sure the lady exaggerates," Olmstead said politely.

They each savored the tea and thereafter the group broke up, with the captain having to return to his lodgings. When his horse was brought around, Adrian showed him to the door, the two men murmuring together for a few minutes.

"Does this newfound friendship with the excise man have anything to do with your plans regarding the locals in smuggling?" Huntington asked as Adrian returned to the drawing room.

"Not necessarily," Adrian replied. "I met the man in London some weeks ago. We attended Oxford at the same time."

"Old school ties, eh? Knew each other well, did you?"

"Not well." Adrian sounded indifferent. "I imagine the captain is rather at loose ends in his new position. Now that Bonaparte is safely put away on Elba, the government cannot seem to make up its mind what to do with the militia."

"He tells me his father is Viscount Hartford," Gabrielle said.

"Yes. He is the second—no, third—son," Adrian said with a shrug. "Good family. The father is not very active now, but he was once quite close to Pitt the younger and the Whigs."

"Becoming an excise man, chasing hooligans through the marshes, has to be quite a comedown for a Peninsula soldier," Huntington observed.

"I suppose it is," Adrian said, barely stifling a yawn. "I want to thank you again, Miss Palmer, for providing such enjoyable entertainment."

"It was my pleasure, my lord," she murmured, aware that his own pleasure made this more than merely a polite rejoinder.

The next morning, Adrian was still at breakfast when Miss Palmer came in from her morning walk.

"Good morning, Miss Palmer."

"And it truly is a good morning, my lord," she said, her cheeks aglow from the brisk autumn air. "The breeze from the sea is sure to waken all one's senses!"

"A great day for a gallop along the beach, I daresay," he responded, admiring what the elements had done to heighten her color. "By the by, do you ride, Miss Palmer?"

"As a matter of fact, I do, my lord, though Anne informs me that riding is not quite the thing for a governess."

" 'Tis somewhat unusual for the position. How does it happen that you do so?" He was genuinely curious.

She seemed to hesitate for a moment in answering. "It was another skill my father thought equally important for a daughter as well as a son." She turned then, busy with the items on the sideboard.

He was thoughtful for a time. How did the daughter of such a father end up a governess? "Would you rather be riding of a morning instead of walking, then?"

"Well . . . frankly, yes. But I am not discontent with matters as they are, my lord." She slid into her usual seat.

"Nevertheless, we shall have to see if you are as talented on horseback as you are at the pianoforte. If Anne is to have a pony, Bess and Geoffrey will have to ride as well. Perhaps you will be willing to supervise their riding when I am absent. You may dispense with the lessons this morning and join me." His tone was polite, but it was a command all the same.

"Oh, but that would be impossible, my lord." She looked distinctly uncomfortable.

"Nonsense. It will not hurt to cancel lessons for one morning. The children will probably welcome the holiday."

"No, you do not understand. I haven't proper attire to go riding. I do not possess a habit."

"Oh." He felt chagrined. "Hmph. That should not be a problem. Surely there is a riding habit in this household you could wear. I will speak to Gabrielle about it and you will be prepared to ride with me tomorrow then."

"Yes, my lord."

Trenville's plan to test the riding skills of the governess were delayed. The afternoon following their discussion turned cloudy, with the storm arriving that night. Wind-driven sheets of rain hammered against the exposed win-

dows all the next day. By late afternoon of the second day,
the storm had reduced itself to an annoying drizzle.

Tempers were strained by the forced indoor stay. The
marchioness was bored, for she could neither make calls
nor receive visitors. Apparently preferring male attention to
the company of her companion, she demanded that Huntington spend time reading to her. The secretary was clearly
torn between this pleasurable task and the more onerous
one that his employer had set him to doing, namely, reorganizing and cataloguing the Abbey's vast library. The children were fussy and hard to please, but Elinor managed to
keep them occupied, even engaging a footman and two
maids to join in a hilarious game of musical chairs the
second afternoon.

Drawn by the sounds of laughter and the thumping of
feet marching to music played with great gusto, the marquis
stood in the doorway of the music room for a few minutes
taking in the scene before him. Geoffrey and Bess and Anne
seemed to be having the time of their lives and the three
servants, though obviously mindful of their positions, entered into the game enthusiastically. He could not recall
when there had last been such pure fun in the household.
Not for several years, at least. Presently, Gabrielle and
Huntington were at his side.

"What is going on here?" Gabrielle was merely curious.

"I believe they are playing musical chairs," Trenville said
unnecessarily.

Elinor looked up then with an expression of alarm. The
music stopped abruptly, but there was no scramble for the
seats as the players had also caught sight of their audience.

"Oh! I am so sorry if we disturbed you," Elinor said. "I
did not realize . . . We can find something else to do, my
lord." She rose and started to close the instrument.

"No. No. Carry on. You seem to be having a good time."
His smile included the three servants who, he noticed,
seemed uncertain of themselves with him.

"Come, Papa," Bess said, dashing to his side and tugging at his hand. "This is a game big people can play, too."

"It is, is it?" The question was directed as much to Miss Palmer as to the child.

"Oh, yes," Bess said seriously. "Dick and Betsy and Gertie are playing and they are big." She had named the three servants.

Gabrielle pushed into the room. "Let us do so, Adrian. I played this game as a child and surely you and Alex did as well."

"All right. If Miss Palmer will indulge us, let us add three more big people to the group." He smiled as the children whooped their delight with the additions.

For the next half hour and more the three children and their six newfound playmates vied to secure a decreasing number of seats. Each time the music stopped, there was a mad scramble for seats, much giggling and laughter, and one person would be eliminated. When Trenville was eliminated on the second round, he came to stand beside the pianoforte to watch as the game progressed.

He also watched the musician and during one of her pauses, he said, "May I?" with a gesture toward the bench.

She smiled uncertainly, but slid over and took up the music again for the players. He put his hands to the keys and they quickly developed an impromptu duet. He looked at her, his eyes filled with laughter. After a minute or two, she gave the signal for the music to stop and there was the mad scramble again.

"Surprised you, hmm?" he asked. "See—you are not the only one who had a parent with rather unorthodox ideas about education. My mother insisted all her children learn to play an instrument."

"You play very well, my lord," she said.

He smiled. "Only the simplest of tunes, Miss Palmer. I haven't your talent." His eyes held hers for a moment, then he reluctantly pulled his gaze away.

As they took up the tune again, he was acutely aware of her hip and leg touching his own and an occasional brushing of their hands as they reached for keys.

Adrian was disconcerted by his physical reaction to the governess. After all, there had been many a comely damsel among his staff and those employed by his parents as well. Early on, it had been drilled into him and his brother that Whitson men just did not take advantage of persons in their employ. If that dictum required passing up even a blatant invitation now and again, so be it.

Temptation had never been a serious problem—until now.

Good thing I am to leave for London and then Derbyshire in a few days, he told himself.

The next day Adrian noted that Gabrielle, or, more likely, the housekeeper, had, indeed, found a suitable habit for Miss Palmer. It was not in the first stare of fashion, of course, nor was the dull brown color and serviceable woolen fabric particularly attractive. The matching hat had seen better days. In view of his reaction to her the day before, it was just as well that she looked more the part of a dowdy governess this morning, he thought sourly.

She had come to the stables this morning in response to his summons. He was there before her and had his own mount, a nervous gray stallion, saddled and ready as a groom brought out a mare for her.

"Oh! She is beautiful," Elinor said. She patted the mare's neck and crooned to her softly. "And you are a very proud lady, are you not?"

"Actually, her name is Lady—Lady Titania, that is," Adrian said, offering Elinor a hand to swing into the saddle.

"The fairy queen. It fits, I think."

"We will go through the south pasture," Adrian said as he swung into his own saddle. "There is a trail down there to the beach." He gestured for her to ride ahead so that he could observe her handling of the horse.

The mare was skittish, tossing her head, and a good deal less than cooperative, but he could see that Miss Palmer had little difficulty establishing her own mastery of the situation.

"She has not been ridden much of late," Adrian said.

"I gathered as much. The Lady Titania has great spirit," she replied, devoting her attention to maintaining her seat. He noted that she did so with the poise of an experienced horsewoman.

He watched carefully as she managed the ride down a steep incline. He was prepared to leap to her rescue if necessary, but she was more than a match for the task. He was frankly admiring of her skill. By the time they reached the sandy beach, Miss Palmer and her mount had become good friends, moving in unison and seeming to enjoy each other. Adrian pulled his mount up beside the sorrel mare. Elinor patted the mare's neck affectionately.

"Are you all right with her, then?" Adrian asked.

"Oh, yes. She is wonderful! I thank you so much for allowing me this treat."

"Good. Then, what say we let them really go? Saracen and I shall race you to that rock down there." He pointed to a boulder rising at the edge of the sea some distance away.

She eyed his mount appraisingly and gave him a look half questioning, half accusing, but she said nothing.

"All right," he said, laughing. "We will give you a count of ten as a head start."

"That is better." She flashed him a grin and urged the mare into a trot, then a gallop. The wind whipped the hat from her head so it hung by its ribbons on her back. Despite the head start, the Lady Titania was no match for the stallion which reached the designated rock slightly ahead of the mare.

"That was absolutely marvelous!" Elinor exulted, her breath coming in short bursts. "It has been so long since I have ridden like this!"

Adrian observed the woman at his side. Several strands of hair had escaped her prim governess bun, giving her a carefree look. Her cheeks were bright pink with the cold of the morning and her exertion. Behind her glasses, her eyes were brilliant with the excitement of the ride. He was breathing hard himself, but he was not entirely sure it was from exertion. Suddenly, he wanted to kiss her and even allowed his mount to move closer to hers before abruptly catching himself.

"Shall we walk a bit, then?" he asked, dismounting and turning toward her. He reached to help her down, placing his hands at her waist.

She slid into his arms and it was the most natural thing in the world for those arms to tighten around her ever so slightly. He drank in the flowery scent of whatever it was she used to wash her hair. His eyes were on her lips.

"Thank you," she said quietly.

He let her go and stepped back a pace, stunned by the effect of her nearness. It seemed to him that they both held their breath for a moment, then she said, "Did I pass?"

"Hmm?" His mind was still elsewhere.

"Did my riding skills meet with your approval?"

"Oh. Yes. Of course. You ride superbly, Miss Palmer. You may take the Lady out any time you like. I shall inform the stable." He gathered the reins of both horses and handed hers over to her.

"Thank you." She reached one hand to push errant strands of hair behind her ears. His fingers fairly itched to perform that task for her. He turned away abruptly.

They walked in silence for a few minutes. Then they began to discuss riding lessons for the children and, by the time he assisted her to remount and they returned to the stables, he thought the employer-employee relationship had been restored.

Five

Lady Elinor Richards was still in a dither as she raced the mare across a field a few mornings later. Never had she found herself so attracted to a man. Of course, she had experienced the usual schoolgirl infatuations—she recalled with no little embarrassment some treacly poems to a music teacher. And there had been the squire's son who had always asked her to dance at country assemblies and sneaked a kiss once or twice. He had been safely married these two years and more.

She had even had a most respectable offer at the end of her season, but happily her father allowed her to refuse that erstwhile swain. Now here, in the person of Lord Trenville, was a man who stirred her as no other had before, a man who would be eminently suitable, had they only met under ordinary circumstances. But here she was—the governess—who could no more command his attention than Lady Titania!

Yet she felt sure there was at least some attraction on his part as well. A certain expression on his face when his eyes met hers. A certain shyness when they had played the pianoforte for the musical game. And she just knew he had been about to kiss her on the beach that morning. How would she have responded, had he done so? Probably like a shameless wanton, she admonished herself, remembering the feel of his arms as he helped her dismount.

After their return to the stables, and in the time since, it seemed to Elinor that the marquis deliberately avoided her. She had, of course, been occupied with her duties, so could not be certain her perception of his attitude was correct. He had been polite and meticulously proper whenever they chanced to meet.

The previous evening, Gabrielle had invited neighboring landowners, along with Captain Olmstead and two of his officers, to an informal dinner party. The guests included a local squire who had earned a knighthood for some long forgotten service to the now ailing king. Along with the squire's wife and spinster daughter, there was a baronet and his wife. Lady Vincent seemed to take great pride in her title and was obsequiously pleased to have been invited to the home of a marquis. The baronet's lady did not trouble to conceal her surprise that the governess had actually been included.

Elinor was more amused than chagrined by the woman's attitude. Nevertheless, she took a faint dislike to her. Lady Vincent struck Elinor as very like her uncle's guest, Lady Hempton, another who used gossip—the more salacious, the better—as an *entre* to society. Trenville's French chef outdid himself with a sumptuous meal that included three fish dishes and two meats, not to mention side dishes and desserts. Afterward, there had been charades and lively conversation in the drawing room.

Elinor was speaking quietly with the squire's daughter when Gabrielle broke into their conversation.

"Miss Palmer, I am feeling a bit chilled. Would you be so kind as to fetch my shawl for me?" Her voice carried clearly to the ladies she had been talking with and to the gentlemen standing near, including Adrian and Captain Olmstead.

Elinor was startled by the request, a thinly veiled directive. "Of course, my lady," she murmured.

"Surely a servant can be summoned for that," Adrian said quietly to his sister-in-law.

"Well . . ." Gabrielle responded, her tone clearly suggesting that she had done precisely that. She had caught the attention of the other guests.

"Truly, I do not mind," Elinor said softly, her tone belying the two spots of color on her cheeks. "I shall just be a moment."

Adrian gave Elinor a look that seemed to express gratitude at her avoiding a scene, but the look he gave the marchioness was a good deal less than amiable.

Elinor fumed as she made her way to the marchioness's chamber and secured the shawl from her ladyship's maid. How dare the woman treat her as a common servant! Never in her entire life had Lady Elinor Richards suffered such a public set-down. Ah, but Miss Palmer undoubtedly has, she told herself. Perhaps it is just as well to be reminded of your position in this household. She paused to take a deep breath before reentering the drawing room.

As she unobtrusively handed the Frenchwoman the shawl, there occurred one of those simultaneous gaps in several conversations that occasionally happen at such gatherings. Suddenly the gossip Lady Vincent was relaying to the ever-receptive Gabrielle commanded everyone's attention. And chilled Elinor's blood.

"I tell you, my dear, the girl seems to have just disappeared. Though 'girl' is hardly the term, I think. She has been on the shelf for three or four years already."

"It is not true then that she joined her godmother in Italy?" Gabrielle asked.

"That is the story her uncle is still giving out, but my cousin Arabella says it cannot possibly be true. The godmother," here Lady Vincent's voice became a stage whisper, "is with Princess Caroline and Arabella's sister is there, too, and she writes nothing of this Richards chit being there."

"But why would her uncle put such a story about if it were not true?" Gabrielle asked ingenuously.

"Why, indeed?" Lady Vincent's tone was knowing. " 'Tis not unknown for females in an 'interesting condition' to suddenly be traveling abroad, now is it? And, of course, now that the war is over, it is much easier to put that story about. But this case is strange because the uncle truly does not seem to know where that girl is."

"Oh, dear, you do not mean to say . . ." Gabrielle seemed suddenly to realize the conversation was taking a rather indelicate turn for mixed company. "Well, perhaps she will turn up with a perfectly innocent explanation."

At that comment, Elinor felt a surge of charity for the marchioness that warred with her previous vexation.

"Perhaps." Lady Vincent's tone was disbelieving. "But why is her uncle still looking for her on the sly? I tell you, there is something havey-cavey about it all."

Olmstead had been standing nearby with Trenville and the baronet. Something in Elinor's demeanor must have attracted the captain's attention. He moved so that his group now included the ladies.

"Are you acquainted with the Richards woman, Miss Palmer?" he asked. When she turned startled eyes to him, he continued, "You appeared to recognize the name."

Suddenly, everyone seemed to be looking at her. A frisson of fear snaked through her. She said a silent prayer. *Please help me through this!* Without conscious volition, she looked toward Trenville. He returned her gaze with interest.

"Uh . . . no. I believe she is the daughter or sister of some earl. Mr. Huntington mentioned this story to us when he arrived." She was surprised at how perfectly normal her voice sounded and how easily the lie slid off her tongue.

"The Earl of Ostwick," Lady Vincent interjected, her tone condescending. "She is his sister. He is a mere schoolboy and Arabella writes that he *says* he knows nothing of her whereabouts, but his uncle does not believe him."

"Arabella seems remarkably well informed," Elinor said, hoping her mild tone concealed her contempt for the gossipy correspondent.

"Arabella is *Lady* Burton." The baronet's wife directed this information almost as a reprimand to the governess. "She is an intimate friend of the wife of the new earl's guardian. Arabella says this story has all of London buzzing."

"Until a new one comes along," Elinor said tartly.

"Well," Lady Vincent intoned with a sniff, "people in society care about one another."

"I daresay they do," Elinor responded. Too much, she added silently. Knowing she had been far too assertive for a governess, she was grateful when Gabrielle said something to divert the entire conversation.

In her own chamber later, she relived the apprehension and embarrassment she had felt. An "interesting condition" indeed! Is that what people were saying of her? And what would they say if they knew that the "Richards chit" had been living in a nobleman's household these several weeks?

Oh, dear. Oh, dear! Oh, God! What *had* she done? If this ever came out, Lord Trenville would likely pay a terrible price in the gossip mill. It might even jeopardize his position with the government.

Peter was right. It *had* been one of her harebrained schemes. How many times in her youth had she gone off pursuing some idea or plan she had concocted, only to find she had not thought it through thoroughly enough? But what might be overlooked in a young girl could not be excused in a grown woman. She had thought only to escape her uncle's perfidy, to avoid disaster for herself. She was devastated by the possibility that her actions could bring real harm to another, especially to a man who had treated her with fairness and generosity.

Please, she prayed silently, *let me not be an instrument of harm to him.*

Surely, though, the truth need not come out. Not if everything went as well as it had gone so far. As soon as she could collect her inheritance, she would, in truth, be off to the continent. There would be no need for the Earl of Ostwick's sister and the Marquis of Trenville ever to be connected in any way.

But that thought gave her no comfort.

The next morning, there was another thought to give her little or no comfort. The marquis was gone. He had announced last night that he would be away for three weeks. He would journey to London to consult government figures and then be off to a house party his friends Lord and Lady Markholme were hosting in Derbyshire. The governess had been given directions in case of emergency. Now, he was, indeed, gone. He had left long before the household awakened.

In the days that followed, Elinor's routine remained the same, of course, but there was always something missing. She missed him at breakfast, though often as not, he had not appeared in the breakfast room. She missed the occasional morning ride with him, though there had been few enough of those. And she missed being able to share some tidbit of information regarding the children's lessons or their other activities.

Not only was the marchioness, the other parent involved, simply not interested in such details, she spent very little time in the company of the schoolroom set. Elinor had observed that the Lady Gabrielle deplored spending any time alone—and she was happiest in the company of gentlemen. With them she was invariably charming, amusing, flirtatious. However, Elinor admonished herself for her critical thoughts, the woman's behavior seemed never to stray beyond the limits of strict propriety. Her ladyship was engaged most evenings. When she was not invited elsewhere, she hosted local gentry, often inviting Captain Olmstead and other officers as well to dinner and card parties.

The governess was not left out of these activities. Elinor was even asked twice to perform at the pianoforte for the guests' amusement. But often as not, Elinor now took her evening meal in the schoolroom, preferring the honest chatter of the children to the empty gossip that passed for conversation in the Abbey's elegant dining room.

Thomas Huntington had remained in Devon. He seemed occupied most days with the ongoing task of reorganizing the library. He was frequently commandeered as a driver for Gabrielle's visits. When no one else was available, Gabrielle settled for the secretary's company. For his part, Huntington seemed happy enough to take her about.

Occasionally, Huntington would appear at the stables as Elinor arrived for her now customary morning ride, weather permitting. Having grown up in the area, he was a most informed and amiable companion on these mornings. Since she often sought refuge in the library, it was not unusual for them to be thrown together there as well. As two people of similar status in the household, an easy camaraderie grew between them.

With Trenville absent, the only other person who frequented the library with any regularity was Madame Giroux. Elinor had initially thought the companion might have much in common with the governess. After all, both were gentlewomen who found themselves in straitened circumstances. In any event, however, the companion kept to herself when not in the company of the marchioness, though Elinor had encountered the woman in the kitchen conversing with the chef in their native French. Elinor did not intend to eavesdrop, but her own knowledge of the language made her a silent party to these conversations which revealed the political views of the two natives of France. Both had suffered from the upheavals across the Channel and each deplored having now to make their way in a foreign culture.

Late one afternoon, Elinor was ensconced in a wing chair in the library, half asleep over a tome on geography of the New World. Suddenly, she was aware that she was not alone, but she had not heard anyone enter. Huntington was seated at Adrian's desk, which was not at all unusual, for he often sat there to work. What was unusual was the concentration with which he seemed to be trying to gain access to one of the drawers.

She peeked around the back of the chair. "I did not hear you come in," she said, thinking it prudent to let him know he had an audience.

He looked up, startled. "Oh . . . uh . . . I just arrived. Did not see you there." He paused, seemed momentarily disconcerted, then rushed on. "The . . . post had a note from Trenville saying he wanted something sent him from this drawer, but he seems to have left it locked. Ah, well. I suppose it will wait."

"Did he have any messages for the children?" she asked. The marquis had been quite faithful in sending greetings to his son and daughter.

"Uh . . . not this time. Guess he was in a hurry." Huntington pulled toward him a ledger in which he had been recording his inventory of the library and seemed ready to settle into that ever-present task.

Now fully awake, Elinor regarded the secretary. "Tell me, Mr. Huntington, did you and his lordship grow up together? You both seem to have vast knowledge of this area and its people."

Huntington seemed more relaxed now than when she had first made her presence known.

"Not precisely," he replied. "Adrian is five years older than I. But I was of an age with one of the girls and I was usually here for holidays and celebrations. There were always several cousins here, too. We had many fine adventures, I can tell you." He seemed lost in memory for a moment. "But Adrian and I . . . Well, five years is a big gap when you are, say, ten years old."

"It is," she agreed. "You seem to get on well now, though."

"Well enough, I suppose."

"How did you come to be Trenville's secretary?"

"The duke, his father, sent me to a good school in the north and assured me and my father that there would always be a position for me."

"I see. That was generous of him."

"Most would see it that way. It was understood I would assist my father as steward and then move into that position myself in due course."

"What happened?"

"My father died while I was away at school. By the time I finished, the duke had lost his oldest son, too, and the new marquis brought his own steward from his other properties."

"But he made you his secretary."

"That he did. Not quite the same, though, is it?" He gave her an oblique look.

"I suppose the position of secretary has less prestige locally, but it may well become very important indeed. Lord Trenville seems to be one of the bright new stars in the government, after all."

"Less prestige and less independence. Ah, well, I am lucky enough to have a position at all these days. At least I managed to escape the trap of many in my class."

"What sort of trap would that be?"

"The army. I might have spent the last few years slogging through the mud in the Peninsula." He gave a visible shudder of disgust.

"The army is generally considered an honorable profession," Elinor said, somewhat baffled at his attitude.

"For some, perhaps. I just could never quite see myself answering to that sort of regimen, though. Now, Trenville would have accepted it with no qualms at all. He was right upset when his brother died."

"I should think he would be," Elinor said, her voice sounding slightly shocked.

"No. You do not understand." Huntington laughed. "Oh, he was upset by his brother's death. They were always close, even though Adrian always knew he was the 'spare' rather than the heir. He was upset at having to leave his navy career!"

"I see."

"Now I, I would have been happy to leave the poor food and cramped quarters on shipboard for all this." He gave a sweeping gesture. "But not Adrian. He loved the sea—still does—and he worshiped Nelson."

"He seems to have adjusted to his disappointment. From what others say, he is making an important contribution to the country."

"Oh, yes. Adrian is ever one to serve his country."

Elinor could not tell whether Huntington meant this as a compliment to their employer. Moreover, she was feeling twinges of conscience for discussing the absent Trenville in such a manner. She murmured something about the time and left the room.

The subject of this discourse was himself considering his service to his country. Was he, through someone in his household or in his employ, the new conduit for sensitive information getting into the hands of the French? His meeting in London with the foreign secretary had not gone well. Canning was livid about the situation.

The foreign secretary had called Lords Morton, Dennington, and Trenville to a meeting. The most reasonable conjecture indicated that information was coming from some source close to one of the four people seated at the table in the foreign office. The only other person in the realm privy to this material was the Prince Regent and, in this regard at least, the Regent's judgment was thoroughly trustworthy.

"So, gentlemen." The foreign secretary's voice was grave. "We have a very serious problem. Preliminary investigations have turned up nothing for the names supplied earlier. We each of us need to consider carefully all persons who have any access whatsoever to any place the information may be discussed or stored or in transit."

"Sir, should we not try to be more precise as to which one of the four of us is involved, however unknowingly?" Adrian looked around the table and received nods from Morton and Dennington.

"I thought that was what we were doing," Canning said with a trace of impatience.

"Yes, sir, but there may be something else we can do."

"Changing the code seems to do little good," Morton said.

"True," Adrian replied. "But we know from our own agents exactly *what* information is being passed on. We just do not know from *where.*"

"So, what are you suggesting, Trenville?" Dennington displayed more than a trace of impatience.

"What if we each had different information in our possession? Whatever got through would tell us the general source. Then we could concentrate on persons associated with whichever of us is actually involved."

"You mean false information, of course," said Morton.

"Perhaps not all of it," Canning said slowly and thoughtfully.

Adrian nodded. "Whatever the French obtain must have the ring of truth to it. They must be able to corroborate this information with their other sources."

"I say we try it." Dennington slapped the table.

Canning and Morton agreed and the four of them spent the next hour and more working out what information, in addition to valid communication, would be included in their individual dispatches.

Six

Returning to Devonshire, Adrian plunged into estate business. Not much occurred in diplomatic circles these days—at least not much in official sectors and channels. Rumor had it that much was being won, lost, and then won and lost again behind the scenes in Vienna. But Vienna was many miles and a social millennium removed from life in England. And so far such wins and losses had not appeared in the palpable form of signed treaties.

Meanwhile, autumn moved rapidly into the fury and desolation of winter. Storms reduced the trees to Shakespeare's "bare ruined choirs where late the sweet birds sang." The prevailing color of the landscape was gray. The harvested fields were brown tinged with gray. Such trees as were green all year now wore green tinged with gray mist. The sun seldom penetrated the gray sky, so even the air itself conveyed dull neutrality.

Whitsun Abbey's inhabitants, like generations of intrepid Britons, sought to mitigate the drabness by warm fires, good company, music, stories, and games. From the lowliest maid to the marquis himself, the denizens of that household tacitly agreed the best weapons against winter ennui were comfort, conviviality, and a variety of activities, the weather dictating that these be mostly of the indoor sort.

Adrian was surprised, but pleased, to learn the children were very much a part of this agreement this year. In previous winters, what-to-do-with-the-children had been a nagging concern of the entire household. Just last year, for instance, a hard-pressed governess and a frustrated nursery maid had been unable to confine childish squabbles to the children's wing.

On the second morning of his return, Trenville was already at breakfast when Miss Palmer joined him. She bid him "good morning" and turned to the sideboard.

"I say, Miss Palmer, what exactly have you been doing with my children?" His voice sounded extraordinarily stern.

She turned swiftly. "I beg your pardon, my lord? Have I done ought to merit your disapproval?" Concern and apology sounded in her tone. Then she apparently perceived the belying twinkle in his eyes and confusion took over. "My lord?"

"Two days of confinement are usually sufficient to turn these particular little people into unmanageable animals. Lovable, mind you, but unmanageable. I am informed wet weather has had you all house-bound for over a week—yet I find all three of them incredibly tamed."

"Oh." She laughed. "Keeping them occupied is not difficult—once one finds agreeable pastimes. The trying part is to find pastimes and games that will augment their lessons."

"You seem to have managed well enough. Geoffrey was most eager in pointing out Madagascar and Brazil on the globe. I think he likes the sound of those names. And Bess and Anne assure me that making doll clothes is much more fun than sewing samplers."

"All three are doing well, my lord."

"So are you, Miss Palmer. I am pleased with their progress." His tone was entirely sincere.

"Thank you, my lord." He noted with amusement that she blushed faintly at his praise. He thought the heightened color most becoming.

They talked of other matters—the weather, politics, his

visit to Derbyshire. He told her of his friend there, a former army officer who was seeking to alleviate conditions for workers and help provide jobs for returning soldiers.

In response to her perceptive questions, he found himself in a far more detailed discussion than he might have anticipated. It occurred to him that the only other woman of his acquaintance who would have sustained such interest in this discussion was his mother. But his mother had not those marvelous eyes which changed in the space of a heartbeat from curiosity to sympathy to merriment.

They were interrupted when Huntington made his appearance at the breakfast table. Adrian regretted the intrusion. Miss Palmer seemed surprised.

"Oh, my goodness—the time!" She quickly excused herself.

Later, Trenville sat staring, unseeing, at some papers on his desk. Once again, his mind was on his children's governess. He had reported immediately to the schoolroom on his late afternoon arrival the previous day. For the first time, eagerness to see his children after an absence had not been his only consideration in his visit to the nursery.

She would surely be there, too.

Her back was toward the door and she was reading to the children as he entered.

"Papa!" Bess screamed her delight and bowled herself into his arms as he squatted to catch her. Then his son was at his side as well. Anne held back slightly, but she greeted him with a kiss on his cheek. All were excitedly talking at once.

"I apologize, Miss Palmer. I seem to have interrupted your lessons."

"Yes. You have," she said, smiling, "but happily so. We have anticipated your return all day, as you must know. We can wait for Odysseus to trick the Cyclops."

He thought she, too, seemed glad of his return. In an instant, all his resolution to put distance and reserve be-

tween himself and the governess crumbled. The usually
controlled Marquis of Trenville was simply unable to
smother his joy and delight at seeing her again. Indeed, he
had momentarily been aware of no one else in the room.

Now, recalling his homecoming and this morning's conversation, he was again engaged in the unhappy business
of taking himself to task. The woman had been hired as a
teacher for his children. He had no right to the fantasies
that arose when he looked into her eyes, or caught a trace
of the light woodsy scent she wore, or heard her irrepress-
ible laughter.

Perhaps his mother was right. He should remarry. At least
a wife would keep him from mooning over a governess.

The next few days were idyllic for Elinor. When the
weather permitted, she rode in the mornings and, more often
than not, her companion was not Huntington or a groom,
but his lordship. The discussion she had found so enjoyable
at breakfast the morning after his return had become a regular occurrence.

She was not surprised at his understanding of political
and military matters—he was, after all, a part of the government. So far as she could tell from casual references
from him, his mother, and others, his position was one of
key importance. What did surprise her was the scope of his
interests. History, literature, the arts—even science and
medicine—all seemed to fascinate this man.

Elinor knew full well that the growing rapport between her
and her employer was unconventional, to say the least. She
had seen a raised eyebrow or two in the Abbey's drawing
room. Not many men of Trenville's class would even bother
with a governess beyond an occasional greeting. Unless they
had ulterior designs on her person, she thought, and immediately an image of the horrible Baron Pennington sprang to
mind. Given her circumstances and the very real need to

avoid undue notice of herself, she knew she should ease out of this sense of familiarity with the marquis and try to establish a more formal basis for the employee-employer relationship. But she also knew she was powerless to do so.

How could she give up something she found so pleasurable? Was there really any harm in casual conversations? It was not as though they were openly flirting with one another! Besides, she thought Trenville enjoyed their verbal sparring every bit as much as she did.

One morning as they were walking the horses after a vigorous ride, the sky threatened yet another storm.

"It would seem that we mortals must abandon hope—for good weather, at least," Trenville said. "I intended to take the children out this afternoon."

"But unlike Dante's prisoners in hell, we need not abandon hope altogether, my lord. There is always a tomorrow. That *was* an oblique reference to the Italian poet, was it not?"

"Why, yes, it was." He flashed her an appreciative grin. "Miss Palmer, you amaze me. I know few women who would have recognized that allusion—or have admitted to doing so."

She felt the familiar blush of pleasure at anything remotely like praise from him. My face must be beet red, she thought, knowing the cold and exercise had already heightened her color. She laughed nervously.

"A governess need not scruple to admit to such, though," she said. "We have more freedom in that respect than do ladies of the *ton.*"

"Miss Palmer!" His voice held an exaggerated pretense of shock. "Never tell me that a lady might be duplicitous in hiding her wit."

"Many are," she said firmly. "But then they have to be, do they not? Gentlemen rarely respond positively to a female polite society labels a 'bluestocking.'"

"You have a decidedly low opinion of men, have you

not?" His voice no longer held the teasing note it had earlier.

"No. Not at all. I am merely practical. It has been my exp—that is, my observation, that men of the upper classes usually reserve their true wit for their own gender. They flirt and talk utter nonsense to women, but anything of substance is reserved for their male companions."

"Perhaps that is because their experience has taught them that women—most women—show little interest in things other than fashions, gossip, or their homes." There was an undertone in this comment of something—regret? bitterness?—that she could not quite put her finger on.

"Perhaps," she said deliberately echoing his phrasing, "that is because the ladies—some ladies—seek to meet the expectations men have of them. A woman is, after all, utterly dependent on the whim of some man. It is in her best interest to flatter his ego and hide her own inclinations—if she has such—to participate in areas men usually view as their domain alone."

"You would have women involved directly in matters of politics and religion and economics?" The marquis clearly thought this idea rather amusing. "Do they not have a share of those powers now—however indirectly?"

"But that is not the same as actually having the power, is it?" She thought bitterly of her own inability to control her fortune because a man had deemed it so, however well-meaning her father had been.

"You would have a woman in Parliament? At the pulpit of the parish church? Transacting business on the 'Change?" His disbelief had taken on a more serious tone.

"Why not? A woman's mind functions as well as a man's." Elinor was aware that she was treading on precarious, if not dangerous, ground. She was, after all, the governess—little more than a servant in his employ. But he was being incredibly obtuse!

"But surely it does not function in the same ways?" he

challenged. "Can you envision a woman as prime minister?"

"Why not?" she asked again. "England has certainly fared as well under female monarchs as under men."

"Not in recent generations," he said.

"What has that to do with it? Elizabeth was surely one of our greatest rulers. Even her predecessor—the infamous Mary—was effective as an administrator, was she not? And," she continued, warming to her subject, "another Mary ruled side by side as co-ruler with her husband, William."

"I suppose you have a point," he conceded, "but it is one thing to have certain tasks thrust upon one through an accident of birth and quite another for one to deliberately seek tasks that are better left to those of the other gender."

"I will grant there are some tasks that men can perform with more facility than women."

"Most generous of you, my dear Miss Palmer."

"However," she went on, ignoring the mockery of his tone, "the duties of the positions you named are not among them. I fail to see how anyone could label the content of a law or a Sunday sermon or a mathematical problem as 'masculine' or 'feminine' in nature."

He did not reply immediately as he offered her a hand to remount and then settled himself in his own saddle. Finally, his words came almost as a reprimand.

"You seem well read in reformist literature aimed at women, Miss Palmer. I do hope these views do not dominate your teaching of the very young females in your care."

She felt a stab of anger, but quickly subdued it and kept her voice carefully neutral. "Of course not, my lord." Good heavens! Did the man think one should expound Fordyce's sermons to a child of five or six? Lady Elinor fumed, but Miss Palmer bowed to the will of her employer.

This last turn of conversation changed the whole atmosphere between them, at least for the moment. They finished the ride in comparative quiet, exchanging only empty polite chit-chat for the remainder of the excursion.

In the days following, Adrian timed his rides earlier, though he refused to admit even to himself that he did so to avoid her. He knew he should be pleased at having found a means of reestablishing a more formal basis for his dealings with the governess. But self-satisfaction eluded him. It had been rather like stepping off a path to trample a flower deliberately. Now she seemed more cautious in what she said to him. Their discussions had lost spontaneity— and he missed it.

As he returned to the stables one morning, he chanced to meet her and Huntington just preparing for their ride. He heard her laughter first as he obviously came upon them in the middle of a conversation before they saw him.

"Oh, Thomas—really . . ." and she placed her hand on the secretary's arm, but, catching sight of the marquis, quickly removed it, and they both greeted him in formal tones.

So. She was on intimate terms with his secretary, even using his given name. Bloody hell! Was he reduced to being jealous of an employee—someone hired to perform a particular service in the household? What was it about this woman that got under his skin so? Certainly the nursery maid—who spent as much time with his children as the governess—did not creep into his thinking with such regularity!

Then two other concerns managed to put these musings into a less trafficked part of his mind.

That afternoon he received a visit from Captain Olmstead who seemed somewhat disheveled and out of sorts as he was shown into the library where Trenville and Huntington had been working.

"Might I have a word with you alone, my lord?" Olmstead asked without preamble and with a look at the secretary.

"Of course. Huntington?" Adrian gestured for Thomas to leave them. When the door was closed, the captain spoke.

"I have just had a hard, cold ride from London, but they wanted you to have this information immediately and it could not be put into writing."

"Well?" Adrian handed him a glass of brandy from a sideboard and poured one for himself.

"I hate to be the one breaking this news, but it would appear that the leaked information has a direct line from you."

"Are we sure?"

"Yes. It was your plan that pinpointed it."

"Bit of irony there, eh?"

As Captain Olmstead had no answer to this, they sat in silence for a moment.

"Any clues we can use to determine precisely *who* is doing this?" Adrian asked.

"None. Canning thought you might be able to tell us where to start."

"Sorry to say it—but I have not the foggiest notion. I would have staked my reputation on the fact that all my people are clean." He gave a derisive snort. "That is precisely what I've done, isn't it?"

"No ideas at all?"

"I have considered carefully all the people who might have had access to my papers—and I cannot see any of them being involved."

"Perhaps you are too close to the situation."

"Perhaps."

The two of them spent several more minutes discussing possible culprits—from the courier who regularly brought Adrian's dispatches to any person with even the most remote access to Whitsun Abbey. Finally the weary captain left, promising to return the next day.

The other distraction occupying Lord Trenville's mind was the family's annual remove to Wallenford for the Christmas holidays. Huntington, whose mother lived in a cottage in the next village, would remain in Devonshire, but everyone else would be going to Adrian's father's seat in Wiltshire for three or four weeks. He informed Miss Palmer of this family custom on one of his afternoon visits to the schoolroom.

"I see," she said. "Shall I be accompanying the children then?"

"Why, of course." His surprise was apparent. "The children will have a few days of holiday, but their lessons will continue."

"Oh. I just thought . . ." Her voice trailed off.

"Thought what?" he asked. "That we would leave you behind? Not likely, Miss Palmer. We rely on you too much."

That was certainly true. But her name had again come up as he and Olmstead discussed possible spies. Adrian did not want to think of her in such a light at all, but the fact was she appeared in his life about the same time this trouble with leaked information attached itself to him. It would not hurt to have her near enough to watch, if only to be able to prove Olmstead's suspicions groundless.

"I see," she said again, sounding rather vague.

"The nursery and schoolrooms at Wallenford are quite adequate," he assured her, "but if you wish any particular items included, you must inform the maids as they pack."

Elinor felt decidedly stupid. Why had she not even thought about the Christmas holiday? Another example of how she had simply not thought this venture through. She had never spent a Christmas away from her family, though for several years the closest family had been only her father and her brother. There had always been a house full of more distant relatives and friends as well. Now she would be alone among strangers. What was worse—much worse— Peter would be left on his own among people who cared little for him. Last year, when they had been still mourning their father, the holiday season had been awful for them, but at least they had been able to comfort each other. Now Peter would be on his own. She felt sorry for him. Indeed, she felt sorry for herself, but she knew she could do nothing about the situation.

She sat down to write Peter a long letter explaining that she was well, but would be unable to join him for the holidays. She tried to make her letter cheerful and amusing, ignoring her own loneliness. She had left money with Miss Palmer in London to accept mail for "Mrs. Garrison" and send it on to her brother. She could, of course, ask the marquis to frank her letters for her, but she thought it much more prudent to await a decently dry day and walk to the village to post her letter.

She was able to do so sooner than she expected. As she prepared to set out on the long walk to the village, Trenville stepped into the entrance hall. She caught his image in the looking glass as she tied the ribbons on her bonnet.

"Good afternoon, my lord." She picked up the reticule containing her letter.

"Miss Palmer. Are you going out?"

"Merely to the village to purchase a trifle or two for Mrs. Hoskins."

"Mrs. Hoskins usually sends a footman on such errands, I believe," he said.

"Well, yes, but as I was going anyway, I volunteered my services. There are a few items I wish for myself."

"The same footman could do for you as well," he said firmly. "You've no business traipsing off by yourself when the weather is so uncertain."

"But it is perfectly dry now," she said, "and it is only a

short distance. I thought to enjoy the exercise." She tried to keep her voice calm. He might be her employer, but what business did he have checking on her so closely, especially as this was her free half day?

"A short distance? Good heavens, woman, it is more than six miles! You should confine your exercise to the Abbey gardens."

"Six miles?" she echoed in a small voice. "But I wanted to . . . make some small purchases." It was vital that Peter receive her letter before he left school for the holidays.

"Well, then, take the gig—and a groom," he said impatiently. "Riverton, see to it," he ordered the hovering butler and turned away.

"Thank you, my lord," she said to his receding back.

Despite her earlier visit there, she had not realized it was quite so far to the village. She had no doubt she could walk such a distance, but it would likely be dark before she returned in this season of very short days. Did he have to be quite so high-handed in offering the gig? If nothing else came of this experience, she was surely gaining a better appreciation of the feelings of the so-called lower orders!

A short while later she was seated in the gig beside a groom from the Trenville stables. He was a pleasant and amiable young man who sang the praises of his employer the entire way—much to Elinor's annoyance today.

"Where to, miss?" he asked as they entered the village.

"I think there is a mercantile shop, is there not?" She hoped she remembered correctly that the post office was located in that establishment.

"Tanner's." He pointed with the whip.

There it was: "Tanner's Mercantile" in large letters and a smaller, more discreet sign saying "Post Office."

"Please just wait for me here," she instructed the groom when it seemed he would follow her into the shop after helping her to alight.

"Yes, miss."

As she entered the shop Elinor nodded a greeting to the plump woman behind the counter and the customer she was serving. The proprietor returned the greeting, asked if she could be of service, and pointed Elinor in the right direction for ribbons, needles, and knitting wool. Elinor cast a surreptitious glance at the other two as they resumed their conversation in subdued tones. She was sure they were discussing her. Finally, the customer left and Elinor took her items to the counter.

"Oh! And I should like to post this letter," she said, keeping her voice casual as she fished the letter and some coins to pay for her purchases out of her reticule.

"Ain't ye the new governess at the Abbey?" the woman asked curiously, pausing in the transaction.

"Yes, I am."

"Well, then, whyn't ye 'ave 'is lordship frank this fer ye?"

"I could not trouble Lord Trenville with my personal correspondence, now could I?" Elinor smiled—disarmingly, she hoped.

"Don't see why not," the woman replied. " 'is lordship is a right kindly fellow."

"Yes, he is," Elinor agreed, making her tone more firm. "But I do not wish to trouble him with my personal business."

The woman behind the counter shrugged. " 'ave it yer way—but this here's a thick'n. Gonna be dear at t'other end."

"The receiver is prepared to pay," Elinor said, gathering up her packages.

Just then the bell attached to the door jingled to herald the entrance of another customer.

"Greetings, Mrs. Tanner. How is my favorite shopkeeper in all of West Benton?" Elinor's heart sank as she recognized that hearty voice as belonging to Captain Olmstead. "Ah, Miss Palmer." He gave her a polite bow. "May I help you?" He reached to take her packages which she automatically gave over to him.

He walked out to the gig with her, making idle conversation as they went. He handed her up, gave her the packages, and stepped back to wave her off before returning to the shop.

Her mind in turmoil during the return drive, she paid scant attention to the groom's chatter. Would Olmstead learn she had posted a letter? Perhaps she should have had Trenville frank it after all. What was the likelihood of his connecting the names of Garrison and Palmer and discovering the ruse? No. It was better this way. Surely Captain Olmstead would have no reason to inquire about her business in the mercantile shop or to note the activities of a mere governess.

Seven

The chief residents of Whitsun Abbey, along with the governess, two maids, his lordship's valet, and necessary outriders and groomsmen to attend three carriages, removed to Wallenford during the second week of December.

Wallenford was not the first ducal seat Elinor had ever visited, but it was certainly the most elegant. The huge, palatial house showed an eclectic gathering of architectural styles spanning its nearly three centuries. Elinor would have been lost several times had the children not taken great delight in showing her about.

For the Duchess of Wallenford, Christmas was obviously *the* big family and social occasion of the year, though Elinor had learned earlier that her grace also enjoyed the season in Town. As more guests arrived and the guest chambers filled up, Elinor had some difficulty keeping all the names attached to their correct faces. Besides the oldest son's widow and child and the younger son and his children, there were the two daughters of the Duke and Duchess of Wallenford along with their titled spouses and an assortment of six more children. In addition, there was an older gentleman who turned out to be the duke's younger brother, a navy admiral whom Adrian obviously admired. And there was Henrietta—Aunt Henny—whom everyone adored, despite her rather brusque manner. Though bound to a wheeled chair, the Lady Henrietta missed nothing.

As the family gathered, lessons diminished in importance, until finally the children were left largely to their own entertainments and the supervision of their respective nursery maids. As the only governess in attendance, Elinor distinctly felt neither fish nor fowl. She wondered resentfully just why she was here.

She was invited and readily accompanied the others when they went on excursions with the children—ice skating, building a whole family of snow people, and caroling. Watching the others enjoy their family togetherness made her acutely aware of missing her brother and she worried anew about his being alone. Well, perhaps not alone in the sense of not having others about, but certainly not in the most convivial of company with Uncle Brompton and that lot. *And,* she asked herself, *do you truly think you could have been with Peter without the Bromptons knowing?*

Scarcely had the family been duly accommodated when an assemblage of guests began to occupy the remaining chambers. In the end, there would be nearly thirty adult guests, plus sundry children. Elinor was informed that her presence would be required at evening meals and entertainments. While she considered it a kindness of the duchess to include her, she suffered no illusions. Her presence was "required" to even the numbers at table.

The additional guests were an assortment of members of two generations—that of the duke and duchess on the one hand, and their children on the other. The latter group included several eligible ladies and gentlemen. One afternoon as guests gathered for tea, Elinor chanced to overhear Adrian's two sisters talking quietly with one another.

"Well," the Countess of Cambden was saying, "I do not see why Mother persists in putting those two together. Merrilee Grimsley has been out for two seasons now. If he were truly interested, he would pay her more attention."

"You know how our dear mama fancies herself a matchmaker," the other, the Viscountess Tellson, replied.

"And with disastrous results. Beatrice was a mistake of major proportions."

"Oh, come now. He was besotted with her initially."

"Perhaps," the countess agreed reluctantly. "A pretty face and practiced charm can do wonders. But let's face it—our brothers did not show much sense in choosing their wives!"

Good heavens! They were discussing Adrian. Elinor was embarrassed at being privy to such a conversation, but she could not tear herself away.

Lady Tellson laughed. "You must admit that Gabrielle has just the sort of charm that attracts gentlemen like flies to honey."

"She does that," the other concurred. "But neither she nor Beatrice had much in common with their husbands. Had he lived, Alex would have been bored eventually with Gabrielle. And, lord knows, Adrian was bored within weeks of the marriage vows."

"I think you are right. He never said anything, though. Just immersed himself in work."

"And then felt guilty when he lost her as the twins were born. Now, just as he seems to be regaining some of his old vitality, Mother presents him with another bubble-brained debutante." Lady Cambden was clearly vexed with her mother.

"The dowager Lady Grimsley is very eager to see her daughter a marchioness."

"Poor Adrian. Beset from all sides."

With that, the two women drifted away.

In the evenings, the duchess provided a variety of activities to amuse her guests—card games, charades, and musical performances—often evolving into impromptu dancing. One evening, the duchess invited members of the local gentry to join her house party for a performance of Christmas plays by a group of mummers and dancing afterward. It was to be a very festive affair. The ballroom was richly decorated and she had hired a group of musicians.

Since overhearing the conversation between Adrian's sisters, Elinor made more effort to sort out the various characters in the near theatrical production that was the Wallenfords' house party. She like the ladies Tellson and Cambden, both of whom seemed level-headed and intelligent. Lady Elinor Richards would have welcomed their friendship. Their husbands were likeable sorts, too.

Gabrielle was in her element. The ladies of the party supplied her with gossipy *on dits* and several gentlemen—two of them quite seriously—never failed to direct flattering flirtations her way. She did not appear to favor a particular gentleman, but Elinor thought the lovely Frenchwoman would not be the Dowager Marchioness of Trenville for much longer.

Elinor had also taken note of the young woman Adrian's sisters had mentioned. Merrilee Grimsley was a very pretty blond girl four or five years younger than Elinor. She had a sparkling laugh and seemed eager to please.

And the person she seemed most eager to please was his lordship, the Marquis of Trenville. She was frequently in his company. If the game was charades, she was on his team. If they played cards, she was his partner. He often stood up to dance with her. That these pairings more often than not were the work of his mother or hers was beside the point—the girl commanded much of his time and attention.

The centerpiece of the decorations in the ballroom was a "kissing ball," a huge globe of mistletoe hung with a red bow. There was much laughter and teasing as various couples were caught—or allowed themselves to be caught—under the kissing ball.

At the end of a lively country dance Adrian was caught there with Merrilee.

Amidst much playful urging from onlookers he was encouraged to take advantage of the opportunity. Merrilee seemed to offer her lips and with a roomful of spectators, he could hardly have refused to kiss her, had he wanted to. And, so far as Elinor could see, there was little reluctance on his part to perform the deed. Perhaps he meant it to be a quick kiss, but Merrilee wound her arms around his neck and visibly pressed her body against his. Elinor felt a terrible wrenching sensation in her midsection and turned away to occupy herself elsewhere.

Twice, in doing the gentlemanly thing of making all the guests feel welcomed in the last few days, Adrian had danced with her. Each time she felt the familiar physical reaction he seemed always to evoke. She was a fool, she now admonished herself, ever to think he might be remotely interested in an insignificant governess. And the fact she was not really a governess was of no consequence. Indeed, should it ever be found out, the result would be a monumental scandal. Meanwhile, his mother seemed to be enjoying success in promoting the match of her choice.

The next day Elinor was returning from an afternoon walk when she encountered Lady Henrietta bundled up with a laprobe and reading a book on the terrace.

"Are you not chilly out here, my lady?" Elinor asked.

"Not really. The sun, weak as it is, feels good. Come join me, my dear."

"Thank you." Eleanor took a nearby chair.

"You seem decidedly unhappy to me," Lady Henrietta said.

"I cannot think why you would think so, Lady Henrietta," Elinor equivocated.

"My dear Miss Palmer, it is my body, not my perception that is impaired. I am said to be a very good listener, so tell me your story." The words commanded, but the tone was gentle.

"You would be unlikely to find my tale extraordinary, my lady." Elinor again sought to divert the older woman's attention.

"Every human being has an extraordinary tale to tell if

one only listens and observes. Now, tell me why you are so unhappy, my dear."

"I am not precisely unhappy," Elinor began slowly. Perceiving Lady Henrietta's disbelief, she went on, "It is just that I have a brother and he is more or less alone this holiday and I miss him."

Lady Henrietta nodded sympathetically. "Being a governess ain't easy, is it? I narrowly missed that life myself."

"Oh?" Elinor prompted.

"I did not take well, you see. My parents tried to arrange a match, but I was able to talk Papa out of it. Then Mary fell head over heels for Wallenford—he was Trenville, then, you know. They take care of me." She laughed again. "Perhaps it is just as well I did not take, ending up in this chair as I did. But, as I said, I might have been in the same position you hold."

"It is not truly so bad," Elinor said. "His lordship is very generous and the children are delightful." She smiled and added, "Most of the time."

Lady Henrietta eyed her companion speculatively. "You are young and pretty. How is it that your parents did not do better by you?"

Elinor blushed. How could she answer this question? "My parents are both dead, my lady. Mother died when my younger brother was born. And Father some time later." She could hardly admit to this woman that it had been only a year and a few months since her father's death.

"And your brother?"

"He is in school much of the time. He is spending his holiday with our uncle."

"Your uncle? Why are you not with him?"

Elinor shifted uncomfortably. These questions were, of course, obtrusively nosy. Somehow, one did not resent them from this woman, but neither could she answer them in a forthright manner.

"My uncle is not in a position to help me," she said. Well, that was true enough.

"How unfortunate for you," Aunt Henny replied, "but fortunate for Adrian. He tells me you are very good with the children."

"His lordship is very kind," Elinor murmured.

"And how do you get on with *him?* He is accounted by some to be arrogant and overbearing, though I have personally never observed such," Trenville's aunt said.

Yet another question to which it was hard to respond. Elinor kept quiet.

Lady Henrietta patted Elinor's hand. "I am sorry, my dear. I did not mean to put you in an uncomfortable position. I adore my nephew and it is my greatest wish to see him happy. He has been far too intense in recent years. Not the carefree young man he used to be."

"That is understandable, is it not?" Elinor asked.

"Oh, yes, but he withholds himself. Does not trust others as he used to." Adrian's aunt sat pensively for a moment, then she added, "Or, perhaps it is his own judgment of others that he does not trust as he used to. There seems to be good rapport between the two of you, though."

"I hope so." Elinor's voice sounded neutral, but she wondered if Lady Henrietta suspected her attraction to her employer.

For Adrian, the removal to Wallenford had brought few changes in his work with the Foreign Office. He continued to receive government dispatches and dealt with them as they arrived. In this respect, the visit was most fortunate, for Wallenford was considerably closer to London than the Abbey was.

During the second week of their stay at his father's chief residence, he received a message requiring immediate response. Ordering a footman to take the courier to the kitchen for some refreshment, Adrian retreated to his father's library to prepare his reply. When he finished, he found no footman available to summon the courier. He carried the sealed packet to the kitchen himself.

As he pushed open the door of the kitchen, he heard voices and laughter. There, seated at one end of the huge worktable in the center of the room, was his courier, placidly partaking of bread, cheese, sweet cakes, and cider. At an angle from the courier, her hands encircling a mug of cider, sat Miss Palmer. The two of them appeared to be enjoying a casual conversation with the cook and one of the kitchen maids.

For a moment, everyone seemed locked in a silent tableau. The courier jumped to his feet as Adrian cleared his throat.

"Thompkins, when you have finished your meal, you may be on your way." He laid the dispatch case on the table between the man and Miss Palmer and with a gesture indicated that Thompkins should reseat himself.

"Yes, sir. Right away."

"Mr. Thompkins was just telling us a most amusing tale from his service in the Peninsula." Miss Palmer's eyes twinkled with merriment behind her glasses.

Adrian raised an eyebrow in question.

"It seems one of their pack donkeys adopted a dog as its companion," she explained.

"An' that devil of a donkey wouldn't move a step less'n his friend was with 'im," Thompkins assured his audience.

"Interesting. Do finish your meal," Adrian said again to the courier. "We cannot have you fainting from hunger on the road." He took a seat himself across from Miss Palmer. "I was not aware that you two knew each other." He tried not to sound suspicious.

The cook placed a cup of the hot brew in front of Adrian and retreated.

"Oh, we do not really know each other," Elinor explained, "but we did meet at the Abbey some weeks ago when Mr. Thompkins brought you a message."

"Miss Palmer's a good listener." Thompkins chuckled. "She always laughs at me jokes."

They talked briefly of weather and road conditions, then the courier departed and the others went about their business.

Was this scene as innocent as it appeared? Adrian wondered. Or, was Miss Palmer an even better listener than the courier supposed? Adrian was fully aware that she had sent some sort of message to London via the post, though Olmstead had been unable to determine the precise direction. That she had chosen to post it herself without asking him to frank it was curious indeed. Now here she was—apparently quite at ease in the company of a man who regularly had access to extremely sensitive information.

Adrian was as perplexed as he ever remembered being in his adult life. He absolutely did not want to believe her guilty of spying. Why did it matter so much? he asked himself. The spy was certainly someone connected to him. She was new. He knew little of her. She was a logical suspect, was she not? But, not her. *Please, let it not be her. . . .*

Then he was struck by the personal interest this silent plea indicated on his part. He was not such a fool that he could ignore his own physical reaction to her. Dancing with her had been a mistake, but he had not been able to help himself—and doing the pretty for all the female guests had provided the opportunity. Even now, he recalled the scent she wore and the way she fit so perfectly in his arms.

Nor was it just the physical attraction. He liked her as a friend, found her to be as easy to talk with as ever any of his best male friends had been. He liked watching her emotions flit across her face, seeing her eyes light with humor or soften with concern. He loved watching her with his children.

Bloody hell! She was the governess. Of course she

should be good with the children. That was, after all, what she was paid to do. And be.

He should be concentrating on the lovely Merrilee. His mother had made her intent quite clear before the arrival of the Grimsley party.

"I have included the Dowager Lady Grimsley and her son and daughter," the duchess had informed Adrian when he joined his mother in her sitting room on the morning after his arrival. "I believe you are acquainted with them."

"Yes, Mother. You know very well I am." There was a resigned, I-know-what-you-are-about tone in his voice.

"Merrilee Grimsley is a taking little thing," she suggested. "Now do not give me that arch look, son. It is beyond time you should remarry."

"And you think Lady Grimsley would make a perfect mother-in-law for me?"

"Actually, I was thinking more of the *daughter*. Never mind her mother." The duchess gestured dismissively. "She *is* silly and dotes on that spoiled son of hers. But the daughter's behavior is all that is correct."

"I grant you she has always seemed intent on making herself agreeable and amiable."

"She has had proper training, I am sure. She exhibits all of the accomplishments one might expect of a lady."

"You have been examining her very closely, have you?" There was a slight teasing note in his tone.

"She would be a very correct wife for someone of your station," she said firmly.

"Correct."

"Now, look." He recognized the note of impatience he had known as a child. "She is agreeable, accomplished, cheerful. What more could you want?"

"Someone to talk to. Someone to share my views. Someone to argue with occasionally. Someone who would be a good mother to my children."

"Well, give the girl a chance. Perhaps she can be that someone."

"Perhaps."

The conversation had then turned to other matters.

Now—more than two weeks into the house party—his mother and Lady Grimsley and the accomplished, attractive, and agreeable Merrilee all seemed intent on bringing him up to scratch. She was a lovely girl, whose studied manner made little secret of the fact that she and her mama thought she would make a perfect nobleman's wife.

And she probably would.

She had certainly responded warmly when he kissed her under the kissing ball. Moreover, she had subtly let him know she would welcome a more private repeat of that performance. But he had seen fit to restrain himself. Nor could he bring himself to offer for her. Every time he even thought of doing so, a pair of gray-green eyes flashed into his consciousness.

After the conversation with Adrian's Aunt Henny, Elinor had tried to take more pleasure in her surroundings. She was determined that no one else should perceive her as unhappy or elicit from her such confidences as Lady Henrietta had.

Elinor quite enjoyed certain of the Wallenford guests. Aunt Henny was a favorite and as she became acquainted with the admiral, she grew to appreciate his dry sense of humor. He, in turn, seemed to appreciate her as a good listener and intelligent conversationalist. Adrian's sisters had been kind, but not overly familiar. The Grimsley ladies were not rude, but neither did they condescend to spend any special time or effort with someone of so little rank.

Only one person gave her pause.

Lord Reginald Everdon, whose mother was a lifelong friend of the duchess, had accompanied his parents and his older sister and her husband to this country affair. Elinor knew he was considered something of a rake. Talk among the nursery maids and kitchen help was that he made himself obnoxious to more than one comely lass belowstairs. He often sought Elinor's company during evening diversions and she had been paired with him for dinner more than once. He was a handsome, dark-haired man of an indeterminate age—mid-thirties to mid-forties. He dressed fashionably and exuded an air of self-confidence.

Although she had initially accepted his attentions as friendly overtures, Elinor had begun to find his presence somewhat oppressive. He often found excuses to touch her as they stood talking, or he would stand too close. At table his knee chanced to bump hers too often for it to be purely accidental. He invariably sought her hand for dances.

At the duchess's grand entertainment with the mummers, he had been determined to have the seat next to Elinor, and afterward, he asked her to dance twice. The first time, he had tried to maneuver them under the kissing ball, but she was adamant in refusing to allow that. Their second dance occurred after Adrian had kissed Merrilee Grimsley under the kissing ball. As Everdon waltzed her around the edge of the room, Elinor was scarcely aware of her surroundings. She *was* aware that he holding her too close.

Suddenly, he had ducked them into a dimly lit curtained alcove. He pulled her roughly into his arms and lowered his lips to her mouth, immediately trying to force his tongue between her teeth. She put her hands against his chest and shoved hard.

"Lord Everdon! Let me go at once," she said, her voice insistent, but kept low.

"Now, why would I do that?" he asked with a throaty laugh. He sought her lips again.

She turned her head abruptly and said, "Perhaps because a lady asked you to do so."

"You are overdoing the maidenly protests, dear girl. You have been teasing me for days now."

"I have done no such thing." Strong indignation forced her voice to rise slightly.

"Come now, my dear. I know an invitation from a woman when I see one."

"You what?" she cried as he clapped a hand over her mouth, still holding her very firmly about the waist.

"Keep your voice down, love." His chuckle held a condescending sneer. "We would not want to be caught in this compromising position, now would we? It would not be *my* reputation that suffered."

She went still, knowing very well how such a scene would appear to others. She might even lose her job.

"That's better," he crooned, his hand still over her mouth. "Now. We both know what these country house parties are all about, don't we? You are not some green schoolgirl."

She made an incoherent sound of outrage against his hand and twisted herself from his grip. He pulled her back against him, his hands gliding over her body.

"Let me go!" she hissed.

"In a minute, my love." He caught her face and pressed his mouth against hers again. "Until later. Leave your chamber door unlocked."

"You arrogant ass!" she whispered hoarsely. She saw a flash of anger cross his face, but he relaxed his hold on her slightly. "If you so much as come near me again, I shall scream my head off. I do not think the duke would take kindly to your behavior."

She knew this threat hit home, for he immediately released her and gave her a stiff little bow. She quickly escaped the alcove. She tried to look calm and at ease as she emerged into the ballroom. She wanted nothing so much as to escape to her room, but she forced herself to do so sedately, smiling and speaking trivialities as she made her way to the door.

That night the nightmares came again. They had plagued her in London, but gradually ceased during her stay at the Abbey. Now they returned with a vengeance.

Eight

To Elinor, it seemed the incident in the alcove had whetted Everdon's appetite for pursuit. She took care he did not again catch her in an intimate encounter. She also locked her chamber door now when she had not done so before.

She tried to avoid him, but it was not always possible to do so. She was wary of attracting undue attention among this assemblage of social elite. She actually remembered three or four of them as people who had been guests at some of the social affairs she had attended in the past. They were unlikely to take notice of someone else's governess, though they would have welcomed warmly Lady Elinor Richards, decked out in her daughter-of-an-earl finery.

It would never do for a person of her present station to disrupt a house party of one of the *ton's* most revered hostesses. Everdon obviously sensed her reluctance to make a scene, though he also seemed to take seriously her threat to go to the duke. Now, he appeared to enjoy playing a game to keep her off balance.

He somehow ensured she was often his partner in cards and other games. If there was dancing, he never failed to ask her to stand up with him, though she had been adroit in avoiding another intimate waltz. It often chanced that partners were able to exchange a few words during the movements of a dance, or he would separate her from others in the social atmosphere of the drawing room. Elinor kept her remarks as brief as civility allowed. His were full of innuendo. One of his ploys was to pretend, for her ears alone, that they were lovers.

"My darling, I am so sorry I was unable to come to you last night," he would say, his voice low and obscenely seductive. "The duke insisted on keeping the gentlemen away. Tonight, my sweet."

Or, "I know how you must have waited for me last night, all hot and ready. I won't fail you again, sweet thing."

Or, "It will be worth the wait, my love, for I know well how to please a woman's appetites."

Each time Elinor would stiffen and lower her eyes, lest others in the company should see the anger flashing there. But she could not stop the color rising to spot her cheeks. Sensing her reaction, he would laugh diabolically.

Still, it had not gone any farther—in part because she had taken to retiring early when her attendance was not absolutely required. She was honest enough to admit to herself that avoiding Everdon's overwhelming presence was only one reason for such withdrawal. The other was to escape the pain of watching Adrian with the lovely Merrilee.

Although she might leave the company early, Elinor rarely went to sleep early. Always a reader, she now buried herself in that pastime. Books kept her mind from dwelling on how she was to keep up this charade for the next several months. Or wondering how Peter was getting on. Or considering her growing fixation on her employer. Or worrying that Everdon might become even more obnoxious.

As it was, Lord Everdon and the horrible Baron Pennington seemed to take turns plaguing her dreams. The dream was always the same. She was being pursued through a dark forest, a corridor of trees looming ominously overhead. Her feet were leaden, never able to move as fast as she wanted them to. Ahead there seemed a lighter opening in the trees and a figure could be dimly seen there. Heavy steps thudded closer and closer. Unwelcome hands reached for her, often touching, never quite grasping.

At that point, she would awaken. Often she was wakened by her own sobs. Fear was a foul taste in the back of her mouth. It would then be a long time before sleep reclaimed her.

She became increasingly reluctant to go to sleep and deliberately prolonged her evening reading, hoping eventually to be too tired to entertain horrible dreams.

Christmas had come and gone with its special festivities of a Yule log, caroling, and gifts. It was followed immediately by St. Stephen's Day, the day to spread goodwill and good things among the tenants, the servants, and the parish poor. The children played hard and often fell into bed without the usual protests. Elinor still spent a good deal of time with her three charges and often found herself entertaining other children as well. Bess and Geoffrey established their proprietary rights to the spots nearest their Miss Palmer when she read to the entire group in the afternoons.

One day just before the new year, Elinor noted that Bess was unusually fussy and her face seemed flushed. Putting her hand on the child's forehead, Elinor thought she might be slightly feverish. She consulted the children's nurse and the two of them agreed to monitor the little girl's condition throughout the night. They would notify Lord Trenville only if her condition worsened.

Elinor's room was directly across the hall from the room Bess and Anne shared with a girl cousin. The nursery maids had a room two doors down. Convinced by now that Everdon was more an annoyance than a real threat to her person, Elinor decided to leave her door and the door to Bess's room slightly open so she could hear the child if she cried out. She wondered if she would sleep at all this night.

* * *

Adrian had never cultivated Everdon's friendship, though he had accorded the man proper civility as a close connection of his parents' friends. As he became aware of Lord Everdon's attentions toward Miss Palmer, he was increasingly critical of the other man. He decided he did not like the man's dress, his demeanor, his views, his attitude.

Hell and damnation! He was doing it again! What difference should it make to him—beyond the possibility of losing a governess—if Everdon showed interest in Miss Palmer?

Because, he answered himself, *you know what the man is, what his reputation is. He can have no honorable intentions toward a woman of her station. He is said to be hanging out for a rich wife.* Well, so what? She seemed friendly enough to him. What gave Trenville the right to interfere in Everdon's business? Or Miss Palmer's?

She is in your employ and thus under your protection. You have an obligation to see that she is treated with respect.

Oh. Is that *it?* He sneered at himself. *You are merely exercising a proper interest in her welfare, eh? No other motive at all?*

He had seen the couple disappear into the curtained alcove the night of his mother's grand party. Had Elinor not emerged when she did, he would have charged over there to see for himself what was going on. Since then, he thought there was a distant coolness on her part toward Lord Everdon. Adrian also thought she occasionally found Everdon's presence disconcerting. However, as long as she tolerated it without complaint to him or his father, Adrian felt there was little he could do.

The billiards room was a favorite retreat for the gentlemen of the house party. One afternoon, most of them had gravitated to this refuge from the female-dominated drawing room. In a comfortable corner of the room, Adrian had been talking for some time with his father, his uncle, and three others. The topic was—as usual—the effect of events in Vienna on British politics and economics.

Gradually, the ribaldry and knowing laughter of the mostly younger men around the billiards table penetrated his consciousness.

"Come now, Chase," Jason Sidwell said with a hoot of laughter. "You must give Everdon credit for consistency. He never quits trying."

"True," Chase replied. "But then his successes are none too challenging."

"What is that supposed to mean?" Everdon had an edge to his voice.

"Merely that your current targets are not precisely the sort one finds at Almack's." Chase laughed disarmingly.

Everdon shrugged. "Ah, well. One takes whatever opportunity offers."

"Even a comely upstairs maid now and then, eh?" Chase leered.

"Poor Chase is feeling a bit downhearted. That little redhead turned him down." Sidwell's tone dripped false sympathy.

"Who says so?" Chase asked in blustery denial.

"*You* did," Sidwell laughed.

"Any time you boys need some lessons, just feel free to consult with Uncle Everdon," that one said with exaggerated condescension. Adrian observed that the "boys" were only a few years younger than Everdon.

Chase snorted his derision. "Oh, yes. We have noticed what great success you are having with Trenville's pretty little governess!"

"My dear Chase." Everdon's tone belittled the other man. "You really must learn more about women."

"Oh-h-h?"

Everdon nodded. "Some women, you see, are simply more coy—and clever—than others."

"Clever? In what way are women so clever?"

"Some women manage to conceal their activities from watchful eyes. Cold in company, passionate in private." The pat phrase was delivered in airy dismissal.

"You hope!" Chase responded. "That one seems able to resist your oh-so-considerable charms."

"He's got you there, I think," Sidwell laughed.

"The game is not over yet." Everdon sounded decidedly smug.

That is what you *think,* Adrian thought. Just as he was about to put a stop to their unseemly discussion, the duke's ancient butler announced the ladies were awaiting the gentlemen's presence for tea in the drawing room.

For the rest of the afternoon and evening, Adrian was preoccupied with thoughts inspired by the billiards room discussion. He was inclined to doubt Everdon's hints of his success with Elinor—Miss Palmer. Why *did* he persist in thinking of her as *Elinor?* The idea that she might welcome the other man's advances was strangely disquieting.

It was very late when he started to retire that night. He and his father and his uncle had talked long after the others sought their chambers. Adrian told them of the spy plaguing his diplomatic work and the government's unproductive efforts to identify the culprit. The older men were as shocked as he had been when he confessed the French agent was almost surely connected with him. Try as they might, they could come up with no means of flushing out the person responsible.

Adrian had not told them of Olmstead's stated and his own latent suspicions of Miss Palmer. Had anyone confronted him with this omission, he would have found it difficult to explain. The truth was, he was having difficulty enough just explaining it to himself! Somehow, openly talking of her in such a light would make his doubts more credible. And he desperately wanted her to be what she seemed.

Having stripped down to his shirt and breeches, he dismissed his valet. Then it occurred to him that he had not looked in on the children as he nearly always did prior to retiring. It was a habit he had formed when they were still in cradles. He liked watching over their innocent sleep. He put on a pair of slippers and picked up a candle to find his way to the nursery wing.

He found the nursery maid bent over Bess's sleeping form. She turned as the light from his candle penetrated the room.

"Oh, 'tis you, my lord," she whispered.

"Is something wrong?"

"We don't think so, sir. But she did seem slightly feverish earlier."

"Why was I not informed?"

"Miss Palmer and me thought to tell you if she got any worse. We been taking turns looking in on the poor wee dear."

"I see." He touched his daughter's cheek with the back of his hand. "She is a bit warm, all right. Not truly hot, though. Let me know how she does in the morning."

"Yes, my lord."

"I will just check on Geoffrey. You go on back to bed, Baxter."

"Thank you, my lord."

He made his way on down the hall to the room occupied by his son and two other boys. He pulled disheveled covers over two of them and started back to his own chamber.

He knew Miss Palmer had the room across the hall from Bess's. As he passed, he heard her cry out.

"No! Oh, please—no-o-o . . ."

Good God! Was she being assaulted? Had Everdon really overstepped himself? Without stopping to think beyond this initial flash, he rapped on her door.

"Miss Palmer, are you all right?"

To his surprise, the door swung open. He stepped into the room and, holding his candle high, looked around. She lay on the bed, tossing and sobbing, "No. No." There was no one else in the room.

Instinctively, he elbowed the door closed and approached the bed. Her hair was a mass of tangled curls against the pillow. Her lashes lay dark on slightly flushed cheeks. In her thrashing about, the bedcovers had slipped to her waist. Her night dress was open at the neck to reveal a soft rounding of breast. He drew in a breath at the sheer beauty before him.

Setting the candle on the night table next to her own unlit candle and her spectacles, he bent over her. It flashed through his mind that his presence might frighten her—but surely not as bad as what was already distressing her. He touched her shoulder.

"Miss Palmer. Elinor. Wake up."

Her eyes flew open, pools of very dark green in the dim light of the single candle. Sheer terror shone in them. She gave a little yelp and sat up, her eyes still not registering true awareness.

"Help me," she cried and threw her arms around his neck.

Awkwardly, he sat on the edge of the bed and held her close. She was warm and pliant in his arms. He caressed her back and buried his face in the fragrant softness of her hair.

"There, there, my love. It's all right. You are safe." He crooned to her as he might have comforted his daughter.

But this was no child in his arms. And no other woman had ever felt so absolutely right there, either. He pressed his lips against the warm flesh of her temple. "It's all right. You are safe," he repeated.

He knew the instant she wakened. He felt her stiffen and pull back, though he still held her.

"My lord?" There was a note of wonder in her voice and her eyes still held a trace of the terror of moments before. Her breath was soft against his cheek.

"It's all right. You were having a bad dream." He pulled her closer and just held her gently until he felt her begin to relax. He nudged her chin up and gazed into her eyes. "All right now?" he asked. She nodded, but continued to hold his gaze. Unable to stop himself, he lowered his mouth to hers.

Her lips were soft and warm with sleep. Then he felt her arms tighten around his neck and she was responding to his kiss with a degree of passion and intensity and sweetness he had never experienced before.

Simultaneously, they drew apart.

"Elinor?" he whispered. He fought for self-control as every instinct cried at him to take her in his arms and make mad, wonderful love with her.

He watched as a fascinating array of emotions swept across her features. The fear was replaced by joy, then apprehension, and, finally, embarrassment.

"I apologize, Miss Palmer. I had no right to do that."

"I . . . what are you . . . how . . . ?" She stammered incoherently.

"You had a bad dream. . . . I was checking on the children. . . . Your door was open." He was surprised at his own stammering.

"Yes . . . chasing me again. Two of them this time. And he was there to grab me. . . ."

"Who was chasing you? Who grabbed you?"

"Lord Pen—uh, two men. And there was another . . . he held me . . . I could not get away . . ." She buried her face in her hands.

He patted her shoulder, feeling decidedly awkward now. "You have this dream often?"

"I . . ." He watched in admiration as she seemed to come fully to herself again. She visibly braced her shoulders, an action that drew his attention to her breasts. Noting the direction of his gaze, she clutched the night dress closer. "I had it in London. It stopped at the Abbey."

"And now it has returned?"

"Yes, my lord."

"What triggered it?"

"I . . . do not know, my lord." She looked away from him.

She is not telling the truth, he thought. But why? Why would she lie about a dream?

Both of them were silent for a moment. Then she asked, "Bess? Is she all right? I should have looked in on her. I left our doors ajar. I did not hear her—"

"She's fine. Nurse just saw to her." He stood and lit her bedside candle with the one he had brought. He felt like an awkward schoolboy.

"Umm. Miss Palmer." She looked up at him and he was nearly undone once more by those expressive eyes. "Again. I—I apologize. I quite forgot myself. Good night."

She nodded her acceptance of his apology.

He strode to the door and opened it, looking back at her. She still sat there, her white childlike night dress clutched around an unchildlike torso. She returned his gaze with a tentative smile.

"Good night," she said.

He stepped through the door and pulled it shut.

And nearly ran smack into the Dowager Lady Grimsley.

"I beg your pardon," he said.

"Lord Trenville. I came to check on my son." She seemed somewhat distracted. "His nurse sent word he suffered an upset stomach." She looked at the door he had just exited and then she looked away.

"I take it your son is all right?" He was determined to act naturally.

"Oh, yes. Merely too many sweets, I think."

"Shall I escort you back to your chamber then, my lady?"

he asked, just as though he were not standing in his shirt-sleeves after midnight in front of the governess's room.

"Thank you, my lord." She cast one more significant look at the recently closed door before accompanying him down the hall.

Elinor sat in the middle of her bed, thoroughly awake now—and thoroughly bemused.

The dream had been different. This time the two heavy-footed pursuers and the figure at the end of the corridor took shape as her uncle who grabbed her and held her while two sets of snake-like hands groped at her body.

Just when the fear threatened to choke her completely, she was being rescued. She felt Adrian's arms around her and she melted into their safety and the comforting sound of his voice. This was a new and wonderful end to the dream. For the first time since hearing of her father's death, she felt safe. And protected. And cherished.

But of course that, too, was a dream.

And the kiss? Was she going to tell herself that was also part of her dream? She touched her lips with her fingertips, remembering the feel of his mouth on hers. No, the kiss had definitely been real, but it would not do to make too much of it. Had he not immediately been contrite, already regretting his action? She was embarrassed by her ardent response. Well, she had conjectured some weeks ago she would react to his kiss like a wanton. And that was precisely what she had done.

When he questioned her about the dream, she had been sorely tempted to unburden herself to him. No. That would never do. She must proceed as she had begun. The truth could be very damaging to a man of Trenville's position. Nor did she want to see his respect and friendship turn into disgust and contempt when he learned of her deceit.

She buried herself in the bedclothes as though to insulate herself from her own unpleasant thoughts.

The dream did not come again that night.

Adrian hoped Lady Grimsley's sense of discretion would lead her to quell her propensity for gossip, especially about the man she wished to become her son-in-law. The next day, he knew this hope was in vain. During the gathering in the drawing room for tea, he sensed that several guests took extraordinary interest in Miss Palmer and himself, often looking from one to the other. When the party assembled there after dinner, it was even worse.

At one point, he saw Lord Everdon lean over the back of the settee on which Miss Palmer sat with another lady. Everdon whispered something to Miss Palmer that caused an immediate flood of color to her cheeks. Everdon appeared to take great delight in her reaction. Shortly thereafter she arose to excuse herself for the evening.

The next morning, after a vigorous ride with several of the gentlemen guests, Adrian sent a message asking the governess to meet him in the Wallenford library. He was leaning against the mantel, staring unseeing at the fire when she came in. He turned at her greeting.

"You wanted to see me, my lord?"

"Yes."

She waited for him to go on.

"Miss Palmer, I hardly know how to begin." He paused to gather his thoughts. Her eyes held his, a questioning look in them. "About the other night . . ."

Her eyes revealed immediately her recollection and he saw the color begin to rise from her neckline.

"Please, my lord, there is no need to apologize again."

"Perhaps I should do so, but that is not why I asked to see you."

She looked her question.

"As I left your room, I encountered Lady Grimsley."

"I do not understand."

"She saw me come out of your room."

"Oh."

"Yes. 'Oh.' She did not say anything to me about it, but I believe now she has mentioned it to others."

"So . . . *that* is why Lord Everdon . . ." Her voice trailed off.

"Why he what? Has he been harassing you?"

"No more than . . ." She stopped abruptly.

"No more than usual? He *is* bothering you then. I shall put a stop to it immediately." Adrian was glad to have something he could actually do.

"No, please, my lord. I would rather you did not make an issue of his behavior. I am confident he is merely . . . teasing me."

"Teasing? Miss Palmer, you need not tolerate offensive behavior from guests in this house." No, merely to being mauled by the heir, he thought ruefully.

"Please, my lord," she repeated, "I think it best if you do not make too much of it. I can handle Lord Everdon."

"As you wish, my dear," he said, the endearment slipping out unbidden. "But that is not the worst of it, I think, Miss Palmer," he said more brusquely.

"Then . . . ?"

"You are overlooking Lady Grimsley. She saw me leaving your room. Your reputation will be in shreds."

"Oh. . . ." She looked thoughtful for a moment then gave a bitter little laugh. "I doubt that is of any consequence. After all, the governess is frequently a target of unwelcome advances in upper-class households, is she not?"

He felt the color flooding his own face. "Not in my family. Usually. And I *have* apologized. It will not happen again."

"I did not mean . . ." She put her hand to her lips. "What

I meant to say was you need not worry about the reputation of a governess."

"Miss Palmer—"

She interrupted him. "Once these people return to their own homes, they will not even remember the Trenville governess had a name."

"Perhaps . . ." He sounded dubious.

"Present company excepted, do *you* recall the name of the last governess you met?"

"Hmm. Addington employed her." A nondescript face tried to take form in his mind, but there was no name for it. Finally, he shrugged in defeat.

"There. You see? It is not *my* reputation these people will discuss—but yours. And I have never known a gentleman's name to suffer unduly when his liaisons with a woman become known."

Adrian was himself summoned for the next interview he had with a woman. As he dutifully reported to his mother's sitting room, he was sure he knew what was on her mind.

"Lady Grimsley imparted some rather interesting information to me yesterday." The duchess was clearly not pleased.

"She wasted little time carrying her tale to you." Adrian made no attempt to circumvent the issue, nor to hide his disgust of the tale-bearer.

"She was concerned for her daughter."

"You mean her son, don't you?"

"No. Her daughter. Apparently, Merrilee was quite distraught to hear about you and Miss Palmer."

" 'To hear about me and Miss Palmer'?" His tone was flat. "And from whence came this distressing information?"

"Why, from her own mother."

"Who misunderstood what she saw."

"Then you do admit she saw you leaving the Palmer woman's room? Oh, Adrian, how could you?"

"Mother, I have no intention of trying to justify myself to the likes of Lady Grimsley. But I will explain to *you*—once." He gave her an edited version of what had happened, carefully omitting the kiss and his own confused emotions. The duchess listened patiently.

"Well, be that as it may, son, Merrilee is in a rare taking. Says she will not entertain your suit until you dismiss the governess."

"She might have waited for me to offer."

"She is young—and impetuous. She is also hurt and embarrassed."

"I am sorry for any person who feels herself humiliated, but in this case, I refuse to take the blame."

"But, Adrian, you have been dangling after the girl these weeks. Of course she feels as she does."

"No, Mother, I have *not* been 'dangling after her.' I know that was your wish. And Lady Grimsley's."

"And Merrilee's. You have done nothing to discourage those wishes."

"I was willing—in part because I knew you wanted it so—to entertain the notion that we might suit."

"And you would."

"No, Mother." His tone was gently patient. "We would not. I will not be offering for the Lady Merrilee and you may so inform her mother, if you wish."

"Because of Miss Palmer."

"Miss Palmer has nothing to do with it." Here he was, lying to his mother. Certainly, Miss Palmer had some part in this decision, but how much of a role did she play?

"I hope you are not fooling yourself in that regard."

So do I, Mother. So do I. But he did not say this aloud.

Nine

The Marquis of Trenville returned his family to Whitsun Abbey during the first week of January. Huntington had returned to the Abbey earlier, shortly after Christmas, to finish reorganizing the library. Adrian praised his work and promptly enlisted the secretary's aid in drafting a series of letters and other documents. Many of these dealt with the business of various estates.

Two pressing matters of government also demanded attention. One was the somewhat delicate state of the Prince Regent's marriage and the split this private problem caused in public circles. Many an Englishman sympathized with the Prince of Wales, saddled as he was with a vulgar, flamboyant wife. Others felt Princess Caroline to be the injured party, victim of an abusive, womanizing husband. Each camp had its share of cynical opportunists seeking to make political hay—and to feed the gossip mills.

In Adrian's view, the behavior of both the Prince and his wife was deplorable. But he *was* the Prince of Wales. Any attempt to change his status as regent could be disastrous for the nation. England had been at war for two generations now—first with the debacle in the Colonies and then the long European campaign against Napoleon and a second foray against the Americans. The resulting economic and social unrest needed no additional fuel.

"In view of the situation, and in the interest of stability,

I hope, my lord, you will support the position of the current government," he dictated to his secretary. "Then end it with the usual closing."

"Nasty bit of business, this," Huntington commented.

"Yes. It is unfortunate that the Prince's bedroom problems spill onto the streets of London."

"Is it likely to affect our negotiations abroad?"

"No reason it should."

"Still, juicy bit like this must be grist for the gossip mills in Vienna. I should think it would make the English negotiators' job more difficult." Huntington closed his notepad and rose.

"The negotiators on all sides are professional diplomats. Prinny's problems must seem minor next to Russia's court intrigues and the turmoil in French circles." Adrian handed Huntington a sheet of paper. "Here is the list for that letter. Can you have the copies made by this evening? I want them in the post tomorrow."

"It is urgent then?"

"Could be. Though not as long as *he* stays in Brighton and *she* stays in Italy."

Huntington chuckled. "I guess that is one way to solve wife problems. Instead of separate bedchambers, the Prince chooses separate countries!"

"The prime minister wants to minimize the situation. We need the support of the people on that list. Can you do that many copies?"

Huntington silently counted the names. "Yes, I think so."

"Good."

On the other pressing matter of government, the Marquis of Trenville consulted not his secretary, but Captain Olmstead, who, having himself just come from a hurried trip to London, called soon after Trenville's return to Devon.

"Since I was coming anyway, Canning sent this with me rather than the regular courier." Olmstead handed over a dispatch case. "Nothing urgent."

"Any new developments in our information leak?" Adrian asked.

"Not precisely. Flurry of activity among smugglers here just after you left."

"You think my presence deterred them before?"

"No. Probably pure coincidence—a shipment just happened to arrive then. But I would wager a monkey local traders breathed easier with you gone."

"Why?"

"Word in the taverns is the Marquis of Trenville ain't exactly happy with the trade in his backyard."

"You hanging around taverns now, are you? Oh, Nate, what has an Oxford man come to?"

Olmstead grinned. "Any sacrifice for king and country. Besides, the Twombleys serve good ale." Olmstead's tone turned serious. "Interesting assortment of people, too."

Adrian raised an expressive eyebrow in question.

"Your secretary has been there rather frequently."

"His mother lives only a few doors from the Three Feathers."

"He is pretty tight with the Hoskins lad and other traders."

"Is that right? Well . . . seems to me Huntington was good pals with Bobby Hoskins's older brother. The one that died at Badajoz."

"Ah, well—that explains Huntington's being there. What about your courier, Thompkins?"

"Thompkins? He was here? When?"

"Couple of weeks ago. Let me see . . ." Olmstead pulled a small notepad from his pocket and leafed through it. Then he named two dates.

Adrian consulted his own notes. "In both instances, he was at Wallenford shortly before." And the second time was when Adrian had happened on Thompkins and Miss Palmer in the kitchen. Had she met with him earlier, too? He should relate all this to Nathan Olmstead, but even as it occurred to him, he knew he would not do so. At least not yet.

"Adrian?"

"This could be mere coincidence, also. Thompkins volunteered for this duty because he grew up in the area. Still has a married sister near here. I chose him in part because he would know alternative routes of travel if necessary."

"Makes sense. So far we have nothing solid to tie him or any other man specifically to the transfer of information."

Or Miss Palmer, Adrian thought.

Olmstead went on, "Next time Thompkins arrives, what say you keep him dangling until you can get word to me? I'll arrange to have him followed—see if he contacts anyone after he gets your dispatch."

Adrian agreed. Olmstead was invited to stay for lunch and Adrian was glad this turned out to be one of those days when the governess took her lunch with the children.

Elinor was happy to be back at the Abbey. In a few short months, this had become home to her, a haven where she could almost be herself. She was glad to put Lord Everdon's malicious teasing firmly behind her. And the nightmares had receded.

Schooling for the Whitson children resumed with the happy addition of riding lessons when weather permitted. True to his word, and to ecstatic enthusiasm from the young Whitsons, Adrian had procured a pony for each of them.

The riding lessons themselves were handled mostly by John Coachman, his lordship's driver who was also the overseer of the stables. Elinor always accompanied her charges, but in this instance, the stable master was the teacher. Occasionally, Trenville came out to watch as the man who had once taught him and his brother and sisters to ride now performed the same service for another generation.

One day as Elinor leaned over the fence watching the three youngsters go through their paces, she felt rather than saw his lordship join her. She looked over to see him standing next to her, his arms folded casually on the fence. That familiar warmth flooded her body when their eyes met.

"How are they doing today?" he asked.

"Very well—in spite of the mud from last night's rain."

"They seem to be enjoying themselves."

"Anne has the makings of a natural horsewoman. Bess takes such delight in just being on her pony that it is great fun merely to watch her."

"And Geoffrey?"

"Geoffrey demonstrates great skill, but he is inclined to be overconfident, I think."

"Now, that does not surprise me. Family trait, you know."

Elinor smiled. "Ohhh? Well, your son, my lord, is a quick learner and ever eager to master new techniques."

Just then, Bess spied her father.

"Hello, Papa! Watch me!" She rode proudly in her saddle as John Coachman stood in the center of the training area, ready to leap to the rescue if necessary.

"No! Watch *me!*" Geoffrey called, as he urged his own mount to a faster pace, forcing Anne to draw near the fence where Adrian and Elinor stood.

"Be careful, Master Geoffrey," John called, taking a step toward the boy and his pony.

In the next moment, a cat darted from the stable and through the arena. It was followed by a yapping puppy. Both ponies still in the middle of the arena shied at this intrusion. John was able to grab the halter of Bess's mount, but he was too far away from Geoffrey to restrain the other pony. The animal reared and Geoffrey fell clumsily to the ground. As Elinor and the boy's father watched in horror, one of the pony's shod hooves clipped Geoffrey's head.

"Oh, my God!" Adrian leaped over the fence and ran to

his son's side as the coachman, still grasping Bess's pony now managed to catch hold of the loose reins of Geoffrey's.

Noting that Anne still had control of her mount near the fence, Elinor ran to the gate and let herself into the training area. Geoffrey lay very still, his eyes closed, a gash over one ear bleeding profusely. Adrian quickly removed his own neckcloth and pressed it against the wound. John lifted a tearful Bess from her pony and put both girls outside the arena. They stood looking through the boards of the fence as the adults took care of the little boy.

Elinor knelt to run her hands over the child's limbs, feeling for broken bones.

"His arms and legs are intact, I think," she said more calmly than she felt. She handed her shawl to Adrian. "We must keep him warm."

"I cannot stop this bleeding," Adrian said, a note of panic in his voice.

"Here, allow me. Head wounds tend to bleed rather much. They often look more serious than they are." She removed the neckcloth momentarily and the blood seemed to gush. She quickly pressed it back. She looked around for something to tie the cloth in place. A strip of leather was thrust into her hand, probably from John Coachman's pocket. "There. That should do it."

Adrian lifted the limp form of his son wrapped in the shawl and carried him into the house and up to the nursery wing. Elinor and the two little girls trailed after them, Anne and Bess unusually subdued.

Bess put her hand in Elinor's, seeking comfort. "Is Geoffrey going to die like our mama?" she asked in a hushed voice.

"No, darling. He will be all right." Elinor squeezed her hand, not at all certain she spoke the truth. Anne walked with them in silence.

The girls were turned over to the nursery maid. A footman was sent for the doctor as Elinor and Adrian tended the wounded Geoffrey. Working swiftly and with few words, they removed his muddy clothing, cleaning as much dirt from his body and near his wound as possible. The boy was still unconscious as they put his night shirt on him.

Having served with Nelson's Mediterranean fleet, Adrian had seen a fair share of wounded men in his time. Never had he felt so utterly helpless.

"He has a concussion, my lord," the doctor said. "I shall need to put in a couple of stitches to close the laceration, but there does not appear to be damage to the skull itself. Head wounds are always worrisome, though."

"When will he regain consciousness?"

"I cannot say for a certainty. A few hours. Maybe a day or two. The longer he is unconscious, the more serious the worry."

Adrian held his son's head still as the doctor stitched the wound, with Miss Palmer assisting. Adrian thought this the most difficult task he had ever performed.

"Thank you, miss. You were a great help," the doctor said as he finished his procedure. "Done this before, have you?"

"Not exactly." She smiled. "I once had a pet, a collie, who tangled with a donkey. We had to stitch Antigone's head, too."

"Antigone?" Adrian asked, glad to be diverted by something so trivial.

"Yes. She was such a faithful companion, you see."

The doctor shrugged himself into the coat he had removed earlier. Leaving some powders for pain and promising to return in the morning, he departed.

Adrian saw the doctor to the door and returned immediately to his son's room. Miss Palmer was still there, standing beside the pathetically small, still form of his son. She had remained calm throughout the ordeal, but now, as she brushed a hand gently across Geoffrey's brow, she turned to Adrian with tears in her eyes. It occurred to Adrian that she seemed as shaken in the aftermath of the accident as he was himself.

"He *is* going to be all right," she said vehemently.

"Oh, God! I hope so!" He could not keep the despair from his voice. "I should never—never—have allowed this to happen."

"Allowed? But this was not your fault."

"Had I not been there, it would not have happened."

"You cannot know that." She put her hand comfortingly on his arm. "You could not have prevented this, my lord."

"I cannot lose him." Naked pain clouded his eyes and voice. Adrian could not have said who moved first, but suddenly she was in his arms and he buried his head in the softness between her cheek and her shoulder. He clung to her, breathing in the scent and warmth of her body. Here was vibrant life as opposed to the predator death they had been fighting.

Her arms cradled his head, her hands caressing his hair and the back of his neck. "I know. I know." Her voice crooned softly at his ear. "He will be all right. I just know he will be."

He lifted his head to look into her eyes, drinking in the empathy he found there. Then, with no apparent volition from either, he was kissing her and she was responding fervently. She met his desperate need for reassurance with gentleness and generosity. In her response, he found a haven. Yes. Everything surely would be all right. He withdrew his lips to look into her eyes again and saw his own passion mirrored there.

"Oh, my love," he whispered, pulling her even tighter into the circle of his arms. He pressed his mouth to hers again, consumed now by long-suppressed desire. His tongue probed against her lips. They parted and she welcomed him with desire he recognized as a reflection of his own. His body hardened as she leaned into his embrace.

A whimper from the bed abruptly brought them to themselves.

Staring in wonder at each other, they parted and turned their attention to the little boy. He had not regained consciousness, but he did seem restless. Elinor put her hand against his cheek and leaned over to murmur nonsense words of comfort. The boy quieted down and she rose to look at his father.

Appalled at his own behavior, Adrian ran a hand through his hair. He cleared his throat to apologize.

"Miss Palmer . . ."

"No," she interrupted. "Please. Do not apologize. There is no need, really."

"But . . ."

"No. Please. I understand. Truly, I do."

"As you wish." Feeling powerless against her gentle rebuff, he wondered just what it was she understood.

There was a soft rap at the door and Baxter, the middle-aged nursery maid, came in.

"Mrs. Hoskins thought you might like me to sit with Master Geoffrey so's you could have your dinner, my lord."

"Is it that late already?" he asked distractedly.

"I must change," Miss Palmer said and it dawned on him they both still wore a good deal of the mud from the arena.

"Call me the instant there is any change," he said to Baxter as he and Elinor left the room.

Later, he sat at Geoffrey's bedside, satisfied just to watch his son breathe. He also thought about the events of this day. And about the woman whose calm assurance had made a crisis bearable for all of them.

At dinner she had been somewhat subdued, but then so had he. Luckily, Gabrielle, Huntington, and Madame Giroux had managed to keep the conversational ball in play.

Apparently, they noticed nothing amiss with their dinner companions.

Afterward, he had gone to the schoolroom to check on how Bess and Anne were getting on. He found the governess there before him, explaining the nature of Geoffrey's wound and easing the girls' fears. Elinor accepted his presence with no discernible change in attitude. She even seemed to welcome his own assurances to his daughter and his niece that their schoolroom companion would soon return to plague their lives anew. Then she excused herself.

Now, it was well after midnight. Adrian had long since sent the nursery maid to her bed, knowing full well sleep would elude him as long as Geoffrey was in danger. Periodically, Adrian wiped his son's brow with a cool cloth and forced some water between parched lips. But mostly it was a matter of waiting. Waiting for a change in the patient's condition. Waiting for his son to awaken.

And with all this waiting, his thoughts seemed to dwell inexorably on the woman sleeping just down the hall. He knew he should be ashamed of losing control as he had. Had he not promised at Wallenford that it would not happen again?

Now it had.

But how could one feel shame and remorse for something that felt so absolutely right? In her arms he had discovered a sense of completion that he had not even known was missing.

Why had she refused his apology? Was she so very disgusted?

No. Her response was given freely, born of her basic sweetness and generosity. He was a human being in need. She gave.

And the passion. Was that real?

Oh, yes. He had not mistaken her desire, her own need a parallel to, a fulfillment of, his own. This was so right!

But you forget yourself, Whitson. Had the lesson not been drummed into him and his brother early on?

"Whitson men do not dishonor themselves by taking advantage of women in their employ."

"Whitson men seek women of their own class—or pay handsomely for the services of those in the demimonde."

Miss Palmer—Elinor—was neither.

The woman just down the hall was not sleeping. Elinor pounded her pillow yet again seeking cloud-like softness to lull her senses. Within seconds, it turned into a brick again, refusing to free her from self-recriminations. Finally, she sat up, her arms resting on her knees.

Why had she allowed that first kiss—let alone the second one?

She knew why.

There had been that terrible need in him, an overwhelming urge for a reaffirmation of life. Refuse such a primal need in this man? As well try to turn back the tide.

And the second kiss? She could have stopped that one. He would have honored her wishes.

But I did not wish to stop it. I had to know . . .

Know what?

Whether it was real.

It?

Whatever it is between us. My own feelings.

And?

I love him.

That was why she could not bear to hear him apologize.

Yes. It would hurt too much to know that he regretted the moment, that he saw it as something shameful.

She buried her face in her hands. She loved him. She loved his wit, his caring, his dedication, his sense of honor, even his pride.

And her very presence in his household could bring disaster to the man she loved.

She gave herself a mental shake and gave up the idea of sleep. She would go and relieve Baxter. She put on a robe over her nightdress and ran her fingers through her hair. She quietly opened the door to Geoffrey's room. But it was not the nursery maid sitting at the bedside. It was Adrian.

He must have been half dozing, for he started at her sharp intake of breath.

"Pardon me, my lord. I did not mean to disturb you. I could not sleep, so I thought to relieve Baxter." She spoke softly but somewhat nervously.

"I sent her off some time ago."

"How is he?" She went to the other side of the bed and placed her hand on Geoffrey's brow. "Poor sweet dear," she murmured.

"I think he has improved. He has calmed down in the last hour or so—not so much thrashing about."

"He does not seem feverish." She straightened already smooth bed covers, needing to perform some helpful action, however trivial and unnecessary. "I will sit with him so you can get some rest, my lord."

"I cannot rest until I know he is out of danger."

"Shall I leave you then?" Yes, she should leave, she told herself. It was not quite proper that she be alone with Trenville in the dead of night. She doubted that a sleeping child qualified as a chaperone.

"No. No. Stay, if you've a mind to. I should welcome the company." He rose to find a chair in a corner and bring it to her side of the bed and she knew she would stay.

"Thank you, my lord."

Their eyes locked for a moment and Elinor was sure he, too, was remembering those kisses. She lowered her gaze to the book he had laid aside and deliberately changed the subject.

"May I ask what you are reading, my lord?"

He smiled. "Only if you will please stop 'my lording' me in private, Miss Palmer. My friends call me 'Adrian.' "

She returned his smile. "As you please, m—Adrian. And my friends call me 'Elinor,' though my brother slips into 'Ellie' from time to time."

"Elinor. Ellie. Elinor." He turned the syllables over on his tongue, testing their sounds. "No. You are more 'Elinor' than 'Ellie.' More dignified, stately."

She laughed softly, loving the sound of her name on his lips. "You make it seem downright stuffy."

"No. Not at all. Independent, perhaps. Self-assured. The name means 'light'—and it suits you."

"How so?"

"You have brought light—and laughter—to my children. They have more fun since you came."

"How very flattering." Her tone conveyed a trace of embarrassment.

"I never flatter."

"Never? That must make you popular in London's drawing rooms," she said with gentle irony.

"Almost never. I find most people prefer sincerity." He paused and picked up the book. "I am reading, rereading, actually, the *Odyssey.* And it is your fault."

"My—"

"Yes. Geoffrey and Bess keep asking me questions. I must be able to respond."

From this they launched into a discussion of Homer's classic, then moved on to other works and other topics. Elinor was glad that, while both seemed conscious of those moments of passion earlier, they were able to regain their usual rapport.

There were also long periods of silence as they watched over the injured child, but these were not moments of tension or strain. The shared companionship of silence was every bit as significant as words.

At one point, she went to the kitchen to make them some tea. Both were surprised some time later when Baxter came to check on her charge as daylight seeped through the window draperies.

Geoffrey began to thrash about and make small mewling noises in his sleep. Finally, he opened his eyes.

"Papa?" He was obviously surprised to see his father. "My head hurts something fierce."

Ten

With the resilience of youth, Geoffrey recovered fully in the next few days. Elinor was glad to welcome him back to his lessons—both in the schoolroom and at the stables.

Life had taken on a curious state of limbo for Elinor. She performed her duties with her usual proficiency. Occasionally, she rode in the mornings with his lordship. They were at ease with each other, though there were no more passionate kisses. His hands sometimes seemed to linger momentarily at her waist when he assisted her in dismounting, but perhaps she imagined that.

Late one afternoon when the children were spending their usual time with their respective parents, Elinor was in the library idly browsing for a book to replace the one she had finished the night before. The room seemed inordinately chilly, despite a fire in the fireplace.

Suddenly she felt a gust of wind and saw the draperies behind Adrian's desk billow out, sending papers flying in all directions. She quickly crossed the room to close the open window.

"There is such a thing as too much fresh air, your lordship," she muttered to herself as she secured the latch on the window and smoothed the draperies.

Then she set about picking up the scattered papers. Some were official-looking documents; some appeared to be random notes. She had no idea what order they should be in, so she simply stacked them all together.

She had just retrieved the last sheet from behind the settee to place it on the stack when Adrian entered the room. She was standing behind his desk with the last paper still in her hand. He stared at her questioningly.

"Is there something you needed?" he asked.

"Oh, no. I was just retrieving these papers. Someone left the window open and a breeze blew them all about." She gestured toward the offending window.

"I see."

She thought there was a note of doubt in his voice. He came over beside her to check the window.

"It seems secure."

"Yes. I just closed it."

He leafed through some of the papers, then looked at her silently. His behavior made her nervous.

"I was looking for a book when the breeze caught the papers."

"Did you find what you wanted?"

"Well, no. I mean, I was just looking—trying to find something new." Why did she feel he suspected her of something?

"Carry on, then. I will not disturb your search." He sat at the desk and began to put the papers in order.

She felt his presence as she turned to the shelves of books. He seemed strangely silent and she could feel him staring at her. She chose a book hastily and left.

As she thought about it later, she became angry. Good heavens! Did the man think she was snooping through his private papers? Besides, she had not seen anything that looked important to her. Next time she would just leave them lying about. How would his noble lordship like *that?*

That evening he announced over the tea tray that he would be departing for London the next day and would then be off to the continent. He expected to be gone about three weeks.

"And when I return," he finished, "I shall expect to find that the lot of you have removed to the London town house."

"How wonderful!" Gabrielle exclaimed. "We will be there early for the season."

"Thought you might like that, sister dear," Adrian said with a touch of irony.

"Of course. And I shall have several new gowns. Please, Maria," she said to Madame Giroux, "hand me that copy of *La Belle Assemblee* we were looking at earlier."

The companion handed it over and Gabrielle eagerly leafed through it.

A wave of panic washed over Elinor. She could not go to London. What if she were recognized? After all, she had had two seasons in London though she had not quite "taken." It was true that before her father's death she had spent several months on the continent and afterward a year in mourning. Still, there were a good many people who might remember Lady Elinor Richards. What if Uncle Brompton discovered her whereabouts? Perhaps Trenville did not intend to remove the children to London, too. Then she remembered the fully equipped schoolroom in the town house.

She swallowed and asked calmly, "Will the children be going to Town also, my lord?"

"Yes, of course."

"Oh. . . . I just thought . . ."

"Thought what?" he asked. She felt all eyes on her now.

"Well . . . that perhaps you would find it less disruptive to their lessons for them to remain here at the Abbey."

"That is perhaps true," he conceded, "but the city offers some unique opportunities for lessons, too."

"Of course." She kept her tone carefully neutral.

"Do you not welcome the chance to see the sights of London, Miss Palmer?" Gabrielle asked.

Elinor chose her words carefully. "I am not averse to renewing my acquaintance with the city. However," she turned to Adrian, "I should be happy to remain with the children here, if that pleased you, my lord."

"It would not please me," he said decisively. "I shall be in Town throughout the season and I want my children there, too." He turned to Huntington. "Thomas, will you join me in the library? There are some last minute details to be settled."

"As you will, sir," the secretary said.

The two men left the room.

Elinor sat with the marchioness and Madame Giroux. They talked of fashions and balls and Elinor made appropriate responses, but her mind was elsewhere.

Surely a plainly dressed governess would move in circles far removed from where she might be taken for the missing Lady Elinor Richards.

Before leaving Devon, Adrian stopped at the local militia headquarters to confer with Captain Olmstead. At Adrian's suggestion the two settled in a corner of the taproom in a nearby inn to carry on their discussion.

"Anything to report of Thompkins?" Adrian asked as the waiter left them. The courier had been at Whitsun Abbey the week before.

"Not a thing. He proceeded directly to London. Kept to himself when he stopped."

"Did he suspect he was followed?"

"I think not. Everything appeared to be perfectly normal."

"That eliminates that possibility, then."

"Appears to."

"The leak must be within my own domain, then. Hell! Damn! Blast!"

"But who? Your sister-in-law? She *is* French. Her companion is, too."

"Yes. So is my chef. I doubt Gabrielle has the heart—or the frame of mind—for this kind of thing."

"Her ladyship does not seem particularly interested in politics."

"Only as they relate to fashions and balls and provide entertaining gossip," Adrian said disdainfully. "And Madame Giroux, pleasant as she is, probably has not the depth of understanding for this sort of thing."

"A bit dense?"

"In some areas. She took very little interest in the war. Of course, she comes from the north of France and most of the fighting took place farther south. And her sympathies, when she has expressed them, seem to lie with the Royalists."

"Hmm. She might bear watching, though. What about the chef?"

"I've no reason to suspect him, though it may be of some significance that Thompkins hangs around the kitchen when he makes his runs."

"Who does that leave? Your secretary?"

"No. Huntington is rather an ambitious fellow. He would not stoop to espionage."

"You are sure?"

"I have known the man all his life."

"All right . . . the housekeeper?"

"I doubt it. Possible, though. Mrs. Hoskins would do anything for her son. Dotes on him. And if he were in some kind of trouble . . ."

"Well, what about the governess?" Something in Olmstead's tone suggested he was reluctant to bring up this possibility to Adrian.

Adrian ran his hand through his hair, utterly destroying

the earlier efforts of his valet. "I cannot say." He hesitated, hating to bring Elinor's name into such sordidness. But, given the circumstances, it was important that Olmstead know everything. He informed the captain of happening on her in the library, apparently in the act of going through papers on his desk.

"Anything missing?"

"Yes. A sheet on the relative strengths of the Dutch, German, and British forces in the occupation of Belgium. But it was in code."

"And you think she took it?"

"God, I hope not."

"But she did have opportunity?"

"As much as others we have mentioned." Why did he feel it so necessary to offer alternatives? And why did he now doubt her at all? Was it because she had been blatantly anxious to remain in Devon when he had announced the move to London?

"Nate, keep an eye on things while I am gone, will you?"

"Certainly. Probably not much going on with you away, though."

As Adrian settled into the carriage for the long journey to London, he felt faintly guilty, as though he had broken a sacred trust. After all, was that not what friendship was—a sacred trust? And had he not come to view Elinor—he rarely thought of her now as merely Miss Palmer—as a friend? Indeed, perhaps his dearest friend ever?

Now, where had that idea come from?

What had she been doing in the library that day? Was her presence as innocent as he wanted to believe? And what had happened to the coded page? Indeed, what were those papers doing *on* the desk at all? He was certain he had locked them in a desk drawer.

And why did she really want to remain in Devon?

Aside from his unwelcome suspicions and his inexplicable need to explain them away, the journey to London was uneventful. He conferred with Canning who still insisted on sending Trenville to Paris to consult personally with the ambassador there.

"This is just too important, Trenville, to entrust to a courier. You must take it yourself."

"Yes, sir. I agree."

"And I expect the ambassador will have important information for the commander of our occupation forces in Belgium, so you will stop there on your return."

"Yes, sir."

"And be careful, Trenville. I doubt you will find yourself in any personal danger, but we never know, do we?"

"Right. The Belgiques have been so close to France for so long—no telling where their sympathies *really* lie."

The journey to Paris went well. Adrian delivered his messages and received replies to be conveyed to Belgium and London. And, he attended several elegant social soirees. Nevertheless, he found the atmosphere in the French capital less hospitable than on his previous trips. Initially, on the defeat of Napoleon, the restoration of a Bourbon to the throne had been welcomed by the French people. Now, there seemed to be open friction between the Royalists and the pro-Bonapartists who agitated for Napoleon's restoration. *Trust the French to be unable to make up their minds,* Adrian thought.

After delivering his report to the commander of the British occupation forces in Belgium, Adrian visited an old friend on the commander's staff. Colonel Simpson was a younger son of an earl and, like Olmstead, an old chum of the Marquis of Trenville.

"Margery is planning a bit of a ball in two days' time," the colonel said. "She will never forgive me if you do not attend."

"Far be it for me to become the cause of a marital rift," Adrian replied.

Thus it was that two nights later, he found himself being

introduced to a number of officers and their ladies, and other notables of this English community in exile. Among the people brought to his attention was an older gentleman, Sir Cecil Spenser, and his wife who were on an extended visit with their son.

Spenser. Why was that name so familiar? Adrian prided himself on rarely forgetting persons he had met previously. It was a valuable skill for a diplomat. But he was sure he had never met the Spensers. Then it came to him.

"It is a pleasure to meet you, sir, madam." He bowed slightly. "We have a mutual acquaintance, I believe."

"Oh?" the Spensers intoned simultaneously.

"Miss Palmer is governess to my children. I am sure one of her references came from you."

"Indeed?"

"It cannot be."

The Spensers again spoke in unison.

"Oh, yes," Adrian said. "And a rare find she is, too. So talented in music—and an excellent horsewoman."

The Spensers looked at each other in obvious consternation.

"My lord, you must be mistaken. Our Miss Palmer meant to retire when she left our employ," Sir Cecil said.

"And she was only so-so in music," his wife added. "We had to hire a special music master for our Penelope."

"I thought Harry was afraid of horses," the husband said. "Cannot be the same woman."

"Miss Harriet E. Palmer," Adrian said. "Was she not in your employ?"

"The name is correct," the wife said. "But how old is your governess, my lord?"

"Three or four and twenty, I would guess."

"Well, there you are," Sir Cecil said with smug assurance. "Not the same woman at all. Our Harry is in her sixties, at least."

"Strange coincidence," his wife murmured as the two drifted away.

"Yes. Strange, indeed," Adrian said grimly to himself. With a huge knot forming in the pit of his stomach, he knew instinctively the Spensers were right. His Miss Palmer was not the woman for whom they had written a glowing recommendation.

So, who was this woman who had charge of his children? And why had she insinuated herself into his household?

Eleven

In accordance with Trenville's orders, key members of his household removed to London during his sojourn in France and Belgium. The caravan consisted of three carriages to convey four adults—Gabrielle, Madame Giroux, Huntington, and Elinor—plus three children, three female servants, his lordship's French chef, and luggage. With coachmen and their assistants, including outriders for protection, the group numbered over twenty people. Overnight stays and changing horses en route had been arranged in advance. Elinor found the sheer logistics required to be mind-boggling.

Apprehensive about going back to the city, she forced herself into cautious optimism. True, there were many in the *ton* who would recognize and welcome Lady Elinor Richards, but she reasoned that most would never even notice a governess. Besides, it was unlikely there would be any occasion for her to be thrown into the company of anyone she had known previously. Having satisfied herself on this score, she sat back in the carriage to enjoy the countryside as her companions anticipated the marvels of returning to the city.

The Marquis of Trenville's town house operated with the same relaxed efficiency as the Abbey. As soon as they had rested from the journey, the travelers transferred their routine to the metropolis. Lessons for the children were to be

enhanced by outings to the Tower and museums. The beloved ponies had been left in the country, but trips to the
park to feed the birds and sail toy boats in the Serpentine
were welcomed.

Somehow Geoffrey had learned that the menagerie at the
Tower of London included a real live "ephalent."

"Please, Miss Palmer, please, may we go see it?" he
begged.

"I want to see the efl'nt, too," Bess said.

"The animal is an *elephant*," Anne said in a precise
schoolmistress tone to the twins, then added her plea to
theirs. " 'Tis quite an exotic beast and I should like to see
it, too, Miss Palmer, if we may."

"All right." Elinor laughed. "We shall see the elephant,
but first we must know something about such an animal
and the others we may see there." She was pleased with
herself for thus steering them into a science lesson.

On the day of the excursion, the children were in the
entry awaiting Miss Palmer's arrival and excitedly discussing the strange sights they would see. Just as Elinor came
down the stairs, Melton, the London butler, was admitting
a guest.

"Lady Barbara Harrington to see the marchioness," the
woman intoned in a dignified voice.

Elinor froze, momentarily in shock. No. Not now. Please.
Lady Barbara had attended Miss Pritchard's Select School
for Girls with Lady Elinor Richards. *If she recognizes me,
it is all over,* Elinor thought. She continued down the stairs
and avoided looking directly at the visitor.

Lady Barbara looked up and seemed to pause a moment,
then looking through Elinor, she ascended the stairs behind
the butler.

There. You see? Elinor congratulated herself. Dowdy
clothes, a plain bonnet, and spectacles had done the trick.
She quickly turned her back on her former classmate and

herded her charges away. She breathed a sigh of relief as the door clicked shut behind them.

Another occasion was much more frightening. This time she had taken the children for an outing in the park. Since it was far too early in the day for the fashionable *ton* to be parading themselves along the bridle paths, she felt relatively safe.

When the three youngsters had expended some of their energy, and much of hers, in a lively game of tag, Elinor sat on a bench to watch as they fed bread crumbs to the ducks and geese at the edge of the pond. She was relaxed and amused at the giggles and squeals coming from Geoffrey, Bess, and Anne. It occurred to her that Anne seemed of late to have lost some of her officiousness and was enjoying her childhood more than she had previously.

A footpath lay between the bench and the narrow strip of grass near the pond. Out of the corner of her eye, Elinor perceived movement on the path and she glanced that way to see two gentlemen approaching in earnest conversation. Sheer terror tore at her, for strolling casually in her direction were her uncle and Baron Pennington. She sat very still, trying to look at ease, and kept her head down.

"Don't worry," her uncle was saying as they neared the bench. "She will turn up soon. I'm sure of it."

"You could set the Runners to looking for her," Pennington suggested.

"No. Not yet, anyway. There's already too much talk about her. No need to stir up more."

"Look here, Brompton. I am a patient man, but this situation is beginning to pall."

The two paused directly in front of Elinor and she felt her heart give a heavy lurch. She raised her eyes in a quick glance. They stood with their backs to her, looking out over the pond. She wanted to jump up and run, but forced herself to remain seated.

"It should not be too much longer," her uncle said in a

placating tone. "I'm working on a new lead now. Her brother will be home for a school holiday soon. She will probably try to contact the brat—or he will contact her. We will have him here in Town where he can be watched carefully."

"You'll not have another farthing from me until you've handled this, Brompton. Enough is enough."

"Never mind," Brompton said with hearty bravado that Elinor hated. "You will have the chit in your bed by midsummer—or sooner." He laughed and the two started to walk on.

"You just see that I do."

When they had gone, Elinor sat there shaking. Dear God. What if they had really looked at her? Two narrow escapes in only a few days. How on earth was she going to keep up this charade for several more months?

Shaken, and with a tremulous note in her voice, she called the children and they left the park rather more hurriedly than usual.

On the sloop from Ostend to Dover, the Marquis of Trenville paced the deck, often stopping at the rail to gaze unseeing out to sea. On the coach journey from Dover to London, he fidgeted, unable to find a comfortable position. He thought long and hard about the deception the woman calling herself Elinor Palmer had perpetrated on him. His first impulse was to call the governess into the library, give her a proper dressing down, and send her packing.

The nerve of the woman—inveigling her way into his home to create a base for treason! And not just into his home. Geoffrey and Bess, even Anne in her reluctant way, were inordinately fond of their Miss Palmer. The children would be devastated when she left. She was equally fond of them, he was sure. Something more than mere duty had been involved in her care of Bess during the Christmas season and of Geoffrey later. So why would she betray that affection by spying for a foreign power? What strange hold did someone have on her?

He had absolutely no doubt about trusting her with the children. No. He just could not trust her to keep her nose out of his government business. Had he not caught her red-handed going through papers on his desk? And he had been so ready—eager, even—to believe that taradiddle about the wind.

Hell. Bloody hell! Admit it, Whitson. Not only had she made a place for herself in his home and the children's hearts, she had also begun to break through those iron bands around his own heart. Almost. For the first time since before his marriage he had given himself up to the sheer pleasure of a woman's company—this woman's company.

Elinor had none of the practiced charm and fashionable mannerisms that had deluded the new marquis several years ago. Beatrice had set her cap for the most eligible prospect on the marriage mart, using every trick in the book to win her prize—including his mother's not-so-subtle aid. Besotted with her pretty face and winsome airs, Adrian was anxious to bed her, to carry her off to the Abbey to claim her as his own.

Within weeks, the charm that had captivated in London drawing rooms seemed trivial and foolish. The musical voice now seemed whiny. The harshest blow had been his discovery that behind those blue eyes, sparkling gaily in flirtation, there was not a serious thought to be had. The lovely Beatrice, charming and accomplished as befitted the season's Incomparable, was totally unsuited to be his wife.

Oh, yes. Adrian Whitson's judgment of a woman had been profoundly wrong in the past. And now it appeared it was wrong again. This time, however, his mistake would have wider ramifications.

This time it hurt more, too. He had himself misread his wife's character. Beatrice was what she was, not what he had wanted her to be. Elinor, however, had deliberately deceived him for some deep and dark reason of her own—or someone else's.

Someone else. Discovering that someone else was vital to the security of the English negotiations in Vienna. There was an accomplice, in fact, there had to be several involved. Eliminating Miss Palmer as a source of English secrets would slow the spies temporarily. Catching the lot of them was a far better goal.

He decided to say nothing to her about her treachery, but shortly after his return, two new employees were added to the staff in the London town house of the Marquis of Trenville. If they were less adept at their domestic duties than others in that efficient group, only those belowstairs were aware of it.

Adrian had arrived home in the late afternoon. Their lessons finished for the day, the children were playing in their quarters under the supervision of a nursery maid. They had exciting tales to tell of sailing paper boats on the Serpentine and seeing strange animals at the Tower.

That evening the woman calling herself Miss Palmer did not seem surprised to see him—someone had probably told her of his arrival—but she did seem genuinely pleased. She flashed him a brilliant smile when he joined the others in the drawing room before dinner. For a single moment there were only the two of them in the room. Then he tore his gaze from hers and greeted his sister-in-law.

Elinor had been overjoyed to hear one of the maids speak of his lordship's return. Later, when he entered the drawing room, she could not suppress her pleasure at seeing him. He greeted her with the same friendly deference as before, but she sensed some reluctance, some indefinable hesitancy in him.

In the days following, he was coolly polite, conversing easily on topics of general interest. However, he held himself somewhat aloof. There were no shared morning rides here in the city. His interest in the children's lessons continued unabated, but he no longer branched out into political observations, court affairs, or opinions about books or art. Elinor decided the high-ranking marquis had reconsidered his dalliance with a mere governess. Well, so be it. She knew her place.

The evenings sometimes weighed heavily on Elinor. Often when the children were abed and their parents engaged in social affairs, the governess would avail herself of the offerings in his lordship's library. Infrequently, she encountered Huntington there completing some task of the day, though in general the secretary was often engaged of an evening with his own social affairs.

On one occasion, she found Huntington seated at Adrian's desk, muttering darkly to himself.

"Anything I can help you with?" she offered.

"What? Oh. No. It's just that Trenville wanted several copies of a certain document—said it was in the desk. But he's gone and locked every drawer in the infernal thing. Most unusual."

"Well, he can hardly hold you responsible when he himself made the task impossible."

"No. He would not do that. But why in blazes did he suddenly take to locking up everything in here? He keeps sensitive material locked in his own chamber in this house."

"Perhaps it was an oversight."

"Perhaps. Well, it leaves me free for the evening. Could I interest you in a game of piquet, Miss Palmer?"

"Imaginary stakes only."

"As you wish."

When Trenville returned around midnight, he found the two of them still happily engaged in winning and losing thousands of imaginary pounds. Drawn by their laughter, he entered the drawing room quietly, but with no attempt at stealth or slyness.

Elinor and Huntington sat at a small table enthusiastically tossing their cards down. Bending over a tally sheet, she made a quick calculation and gave a carefree laugh.

"You win this one, Thomas, but you still owe me two thousand three hundred forty-two pounds. Oh! Good evening, my lord," she said, catching sight of Adrian in the doorway.

"You two seem in high spirits." He noted her use of Huntington's first name and the comfortable atmosphere between them. His immediate reaction was suspicious resentment, but he refused to allow it to show.

"Miss Palmer has a wicked way with the cards," Huntington said genially. "She has just won a fortune from me."

"I am sure you meant to say 'won her fortune back,' " Elinor said. "You do remember that I lost for the entire first hour of play."

So, the two of them had been playing for some time. Was there more between them than harmlessly passing time? Had the secretary had access to those sweet lips? He mentally shook himself.

What was this? Jealous of the favors of an unscrupulous spy?

You cannot be sure she is guilty. There may be an innocent explanation for what she did.

Hah! And maybe pigs fly.

"Well, carry on," he said aloud, turning reluctantly to leave the room. He paused. "Did you copy those things I wanted, Thomas?"

"No, sir. They were not on the desk as you said and the drawers were locked."

"Blast!" Adrian pressed the heel of his hand against his forehead. "Sorry. I forgot. They must be done first thing in the morning, though."

"Yes, sir."

As Adrian proceeded down the hall to the library, he heard Elinor bid a good night first to her fellow player, and then to the footman in the hall as she ascended the stairs. He waited until he was sure she could not hear, then ordered the footman into the library.

"Anything yet, Graham?" he asked, motioning the man to a chair and taking another himself.

"No, my lord. She's taken the children to a museum and to the park. Went shopping on her off afternoon. Took a maid with her and bought stockings and ribbons. Browsed in one of those lending libraries. Didn't speak to anybody but shopkeepers, the museum curator, and the maid."

"Did anyone approach her?"

"No, sir, not that I saw."

"No chance for her to have passed information? What about the maid?"

"Nothing. The maid was with her the whole time—nor have either of them left this house alone."

"What about Jones—has he observed anything suspicious?"

"She hasn't been near the stables, my lord."

"Damn! She must make contact somehow. Inform your superiors at Bow Street that we need two or three more men to hang around the street discreetly and follow anyone who leaves this house other than her ladyship or me. Can't risk your being recognized, you know."

"Yes, sir. What if they don't leave afoot?"

"Arrange to have some sort of conveyance available. Something unobtrusive. A peddler's cart, perhaps."

" 'Twill be done on the morrow, my lord."

"You mean today," Adrian said with a rueful glance at the ormolu clock on the mantel. "Thank you, Graham. Oh! Have Jones find out where John Coachman delivered her and picked her up after her interview for the governess job."

"Yes, sir."

When Graham left, Adrian sat musing. Everything

seemed so innocent in "Miss Palmer's" behavior. Yet she had lied about her identity and her documents had been falsified. A closer inspection of them on his return from Belgium revealed very subtle alterations in otherwise authentic documents. How had this impostor obtained the real Miss Palmer's credentials?

This impostor? Was that how he really thought of her? She is still Elinor. Elinor—of the laughing gray-green eyes. Elinor—whose loving care had nursed Bess and Geoffrey, who had perceived a young girl's loneliness in Anne. Elinor—whose passionate response to his kiss had ignited such desire in him. Even now, he fought the impulse to charge up to her room and demand the truth from her; to tell her it was all right, whatever she was involved in, he could handle.

He shook his head. How gullible could he be? So she liked children. So she responded to a kiss. He had no business falling in love with someone who had deliberately misrepresented herself to him.

Falling in love? My God. Was that it? Had he come so close to allowing his own emotions to get in the way of sworn duty? A spy worms her way into his personal world and what is his response? He—the cool diplomat, dedicated protector of his country—he wants to take her in his arms, comfort her, protect her, bury himself in her.

But who was she?

He could not just confront her; that might jeopardize efforts to apprehend the entire spy ring. Hmm. The real Miss Palmer might provide a clue. But where was she to be found? What if she were dead? Spenser had said she was an old woman when she left his employ.

He would set Bow Street on this, too.

The Marquis of Trenville's town house boasted not only its own private stable and carriage house, but a large, well-tended garden in the rear. Access to the stables by carriage was on a back street and a footpath extended through the garden to the rear entrance of the residence.

The garden was a favorite sanctuary for Elinor. In late February, the afternoon sun valiantly extended warming rays. Colorful tulips and daffodils complemented the perfume of hyacinths. She drank in the sensual beauty, sharply aware of the contrast between nature's cheerful renewal and her own despair.

Prior to his return, she had thought seriously of telling Adrian the truth and asking his help. Surely, those kisses bespoke some fondness, some caring on his part, though she was not so foolish as to think he loved her. Still, the beginnings of a true friendship seemed to have permeated the strictures of the employer-employee relationship.

This *had* been her thinking. Now, she was not so sure. He seemed more aloof. Several times she had caught him looking at her questioningly, even suspiciously. If her eyes chanced to meet his, he would look away or smile a bland say-nothing smile with little warmth in his gaze.

It was probably only a matter of time until her uncle found her. Had he not said he had some new leads? Pure chance had kept Lady Barbara from recognizing her. She might not be so lucky the next time. If Brompton found her in the Trenville household, what would stop him from stirring up mischief harmful to these people—one, in particular, whom she had grown to love? She had to leave. And she had to get word to Peter.

She sat in the garden penning a note to her brother which she would herself deliver to Miss Palmer, who, in turn, would have Henderson see it delivered to the young earl at the Ostwick town house. She held the writing paper against a book she also thought to read as she labored over the wording. After three false starts, she thought she had the right tone of confidence and determination. Lord knew what Peter would do if he sensed her despair and, indeed, her danger.

She felt so utterly helpless. Lady Elinor Richards had never been one of those fluttery, helpless females. She was a take-charge type of person. Determined. Efficient. Decisive. Now she knew not where to turn. Taking a position as governess had seemed such a perfect solution to her problems.

It was, for *you,* she admonished herself, but you did not consider the consequences, did you?

Well, how could I know then, she answered herself, that I would fall in love with him—that his children would become as dear to me as Peter?

You could not, but you might have given a thought to the welfare of others when you were exposed. If you were exposed.

I simply have to leave before that happens.

Running away again, eh?

What choice do I have? If I am discovered here, the resulting scandal would probably force Adrian into offering for me. *I will not have Pennington and I will not,* she told herself fiercely, *have a man who has been coerced into having me, no matter how much I want him.*

She thought the tears were only inward, but now she felt them well and slip onto her cheeks. She swiped at them impatiently with her fingertips and dropped her book and papers in the process just as she heard the crunch of footsteps on the graveled path from the stables. Maybe whoever it was would not see her.

But he did.

Adrian stopped before her and bent to pick up the book and papers, but she hastily retrieved them herself, carefully placing the papers inside the book.

"Miss Palmer? Elinor, has something upset you?"

Was she upset? Of course not. Her whole life was disintegrating, but the intrepid Elinor Richards was not upset.

"No, my lord." She managed to keep her voice calm. "I was merely indulging in a moment of self-pity."

"Somehow that does not seem in character for you." Without invitation, he sat next to her and put an arm around her shoulder in a friendly gesture. "If there is anything I can do, you've only to ask, you know."

"Th—thank you, my lord." She wanted to nestle into the warmth of his encircling arm, but steeled herself against doing so. She wiped her eyes with the back of her hand in a childlike gesture. "I'll be all right. You must not concern yourself."

"I thought we agreed on 'Elinor' and 'Adrian' in private," he said softly. He lifted her chin and forced her to look at him. The expression in his eyes deepened with compassion—and something else. "Please let me help," he whispered.

He held her gaze for a long moment. Sympathy, questioning, a degree of pain shone in his eyes. Then with a soft groan, he lowered his mouth to hers. His lips were insistent, demanding, but firm and tender, offering comfort and refuge. For an instant she gave herself up to the haven he offered, wanting the perfection of this moment to go on forever. She kissed him back without thinking to restrain the longing and heartache of recent weeks.

Abruptly, she twisted away.

"I . . . you can't." She tried to stifle the sob in her voice. She looked into his eyes, willing him to see her love, knowing he would despise her when he learned the truth of her deception. "Oh, Adrian. I am so sorry."

Clutching the book, she nearly ran into the house.

Adrian sat stunned for a moment. He certainly had not intended to kiss her again, but he could not help himself. The instant he had seen her silently weeping, all his resolve

to catch a spy had simply disappeared. Elinor—his Elinor—
was hurting and needed comforting. Nothing else mattered.

But she had rejected his help. Reluctantly, perhaps, but
rejected all the same. He rose and ran his hand through his
hair in frustrated resignation.

Bloody hell! Now, what?

Then he spied the paper under the bench. There were
splotches and cross-outs and it was unfinished. Reading it
was an invasion of another's privacy, but was he not supposed to be investigating a spy ring?

He was totally unprepared for the sheer pain the unfinished missive brought him.

Dearest Peter,

*I love you and I miss you fearfully, but you must
not try to contact me. It is too dangerous. They
monitor every move. Be patient. We will be together
soon. A few more weeks and I . . .*

Twelve

Still frightened by her near encounter with her uncle, Elinor set out to visit Miss Palmer on her next free half day. Eventually, Peter would remember how close she had been to the governess and that Miss Palmer now lived in London. If Peter worried about his sister—and she had no doubt that he did—he would surely pursue that line of inquiry. She must try to forestall his doing so.

Melton, Trenville's London butler, was in the foyer as she came down the stairs in her bonnet and pelisse. He glanced up.

"Are you going out, Miss Palmer?"

"Yes, I am. I shall be gone quite some time."

"I will send Aggie with you—or a footman."

"Please do not trouble yourself. I shall only walk in the park and I will return by tea time."

"His lordship will not countenance your going out alone," the butler warned.

"You are probably right, but it will be on my head, not yours, will it not?" She smiled to take the sting out of this rebuff as she pulled on her gloves and swept through the door.

The lies come "trippingly on the tongue," don't they? she asked herself as she made her way down the street. Despite this twinge of conscience, she quite enjoyed being out in the fresh air with no worry of a child dashing into danger. The sheer freedom of the moment was exhilarating.

She walked a few blocks before feeling secure from any eyes belonging to Trenville House. Then, trying to act as though she hired public conveyances as a matter of habit, she hailed a hackney cab.

"Be ye sure yuh've the blunt to go that far?" the driver asked suspiciously, taking in her plain apparel.

"I assure you that I have," she said in her most officious schoolroom tone.

"Aw right. Keep yer lid on." He clambered down to help her into the carriage. "Man's got to look out for hisself," he muttered.

Elinor made no reply. She noted the bustle on the streets as the cab wove through the busy traffic which submitted only to such control as various drivers could exert in pursuing their own ends. Shouts and curses of drivers mingled with occasional jeers from the sidelines. Iron wheels and horses' hooves on cobblestones, along with jingling harnesses, added to the din. Riding in an open carriage provided no protection from the assault to one's ears—or one's nose. In the better neighborhoods, civic efforts had worked to clean the streets somewhat, but where commerce flourished and in the poorer sections, the blended smells of rotting vegetation, sewage, cooking, animals—along with others unidentifiable—overwhelmed the occasional fragrance of spring flowers. *So much for fresh air,* Elinor thought ruefully.

Miss Palmer greeted her one-time charge warmly, but with surprise and concern. After initial greetings, she called for Henderson to serve refreshments.

"Are you sure it is all right for you to be here?" she asked in a worried tone.

"Not absolutely sure," Elinor admitted, "but I must have this note delivered to Peter. Here in London, I cannot be certain he will receive it if I post it. I am sure my uncle controls the staff in London as he does at Ostwick."

"I will have Henderson deliver it into no other hands but your brother's." Miss Palmer laid the letter on a side table. "Now," she said, busying herself with the tray, "how are you faring otherwise? Is the disguise working?"

"Oh, Miss Palmer, I have made such a terrible mistake!" Overcome by the enormity of her situation and being at last able to let her guard down fully, Elinor burst into tears.

Immediately, Miss Palmer moved to the settee and put her arms around the younger woman. "There, there, my lady. It cannot be so very bad."

"But . . . it . . . is," Elinor said between sobs. She cried into Miss Palmer's comforting shoulder for a few moments. Then she straightened and dabbed at her eyes with a handkerchief her friend offered. "I never lose control this way."

"I know." Miss Palmer patted Elinor's shoulder and waited for her to continue.

"I did not realize . . . All I wanted was to escape Uncle Brompton's plotting. And now if it ever gets out—oh, Miss Palmer, what have I done?"

"I think you must begin at the beginning and tell me all."

Through occasional sniffs, Elinor told her of life at the Abbey, of the Christmas visit, and of the children. She told Miss Palmer of nursing Bess through her illness and Geoffrey through his injury and of Anne's development from a bossy little know-all to a more caring person with confidence in her achievements. She also related her near encounters with her former school friend and her uncle.

"You have developed a deep fondness for these children, have you not?"

"Yes. Is that so surprising?"

"Not at all." Miss Palmer gave her a quick, but intense hug. "You were ever wont to strong attachments." She paused. "And what of the marquis? Have you developed an attachment for him, too?"

There was no reproach in the question, but Elinor could feel the warmth flooding her cheeks.

"I never could keep anything from you, could I? Yes, I fear I have. And therein lies much of the problem. I would not have Adrian, Lord Trenville, harmed by my actions."

"How might he be harmed?"

"Think how the *ton* would feast at the trough of scandal should my identity become known!"

"That, of course, was always a danger, was it not?"

"Yes, but it is different now."

"I see." Miss Palmer looked at her thoughtfully. "And Lord Trenville? Are his affections engaged?"

"I—I am not sure." She blushed again, remembering his kisses. "I—I think he is not totally indifferent to me, but—oh, can you not see? It does not signify!"

"I should think his feelings would signify very much indeed." Miss Palmer's tone was gentle, but wry.

"Under ordinary circumstances . . . if we had met in a ballroom . . . but as it is, his position in society—indeed, his mission with the government—might be endangered. And once he learns how I have deceived him . . ." Her voice trailed off in despair.

"Perhaps you underestimate his lordship."

"No, I think not. He takes his responsibilities, his sense of honor, very seriously."

"What if you confided in him?"

"I cannot do that."

"Why?"

"I could not bear to see his disgust of me. Nor can I burden him with my problems."

"Pride?"

"Perhaps a little." Then she added in a more vehement tone, "But I refuse to be an instrument society can use against him. Nor would I have him approach me out of a sense of obligation. There is some degree of pride in that, I suppose."

"So what do you plan to do?"

"I simply do not know. But I must do something—and soon. Here in the city there is too much danger of my being recognized eventually. Had that been Elizabeth Wentworth rather than Barbara Harrington visiting the marchioness, you can be sure it would be all over now."

"I suppose there is no question of Trenville's returning to the country?"

"Not until the season is over."

"And it is only just beginning."

"I fear I shall have to give notice and leave."

"Where will you go?"

"My father had an aunt in Northern Scotland. Mary Kincannon MacGregor. I have never met her—she was estranged from the family. Perhaps she can be persuaded to take me in, assuming she is still alive. It would be for only a few more weeks."

"The Highlands?" Clearly, Miss Palmer equated that part of her native island with the moon or the wilderness of the Colonies.

"The Highlands." Elinor smiled for the first time. "I shall write her immediately and hope for the best. I could have a response in about a month, could I not?"

"I suppose so." Miss Palmer still sounded dubious.

Elinor patted her hand. "Now don't you worry. I shall come about. I feel better for having talked with you. I must go. I promised to be back by tea time."

Late that evening, after the rest of the household had long since retired, Adrian sat in the library listening to Graham's report.

"You say she went to the same address John Coachman took her to?"

"Musta been. 'Twas the same street. Respectable neighborhood. House has four apartments. Two of 'em let by tradesmen's families and two by widows of tradesmen."

"Hmm. Find out who those people are—and the names of any adult living with them. Those widows may have companions."

"Yes, sir. I've the names of the persons who actually rent the establishments, but they ain't very helpful, I'm thinkin'. Benton, Neville, Garrison, and Baker."

"None rings a bell. Neville could be French, though. Keep on it. We've not much to go on. Anything else?"

"Well, I'm not sure, my lord. There was a feller seemed mighty interested in that house. Just loitering about."

"Did Miss Palmer make contact with him?"

"No, sir. Not that I could see anyways. She come out with what seemed to be a manservant who hailed a hackney for her. This other feller followed the hack, but as I told you, I lost 'em in the traffic near Piccadilly."

"Damn! He may be the contact."

"I'm sorry, my lord."

"Never mind. You did well. Just keep at it—all of you."

Adrian sat there long after the servant-investigator had left. With whom had she actually met? If the man on the street was her contact, why had she visited the house alone? Something did not add up here.

Had she gone to meet her lover—this mysterious Peter? But hadn't that fragment of a note said it was "too dangerous" for them to meet? Was Peter the man on the street? Was he the contact?

Peter. Pierre. Was there a connection somehow with the spy they had already unearthed?

Oh, Adrian. I am so sorry. Her words echoed in the caverns of his mind. He knew the regret was genuine. Her response to his kiss was genuine, too. How could she react with such passion to him when she had just been penning a note to a lover?

I am so sorry.

Sorry about what? Sorry she could not love him? Sorry about her deception? If she were indeed "sorry," why did she continue to spy for a foreign power? Who had such a hold on her?

I am so sorry.

Well, lady, I am sorry, too. You and I might have had something pretty wonderful.

He heaved an inward sigh of regret and, straightening his shoulders, made his way up the stairs to check on the children before he retired. As he reached the landing of the floor on which family and guest bedchambers were located, including his own, he observed the figure of his secretary near the room assigned to him at the far end of the hallway. Huntington saw him, hesitated momentarily, then, with a wave of his hand, entered his own room and closed the door.

Adrian frowned. What was Huntington doing out and about at such an ungodly hour? He was not dressed to have just come in from a social engagement. Or had he had a "social engagement" with a member of the Trenville staff? The governess, perhaps?

Good God. You are ready to suspect her at every turn, aren't you? Besides, Huntington knows very well the rules regarding Whitson employees. It is not likely he would risk his position to carry on a clandestine affair right under your nose.

He shrugged and continued climbing the stairs to the next floor which featured the children's rooms—their bedrooms, playroom, schoolroom, and chambers for the nurse and governess. He found Elinor seated on the edge of his daughter's bed holding the sobbing child tightly to her. A lamp, its wick turned low, shed a dim light.

"It's all right, darling," he heard Elinor murmur. "It's all right. It was only a dream."

Instantly he took in the scene and recalled the earlier

time when Elinor had herself needed the sort of comforting she now extended to Bess. And he recalled how she had felt in his arms then, too. Bess had begun to quiet and pull back from Elinor when she spied her father.

"Oh, Papa. I had a bad dream." She reached for him and quickly wrapped her arms and legs around him as he held her.

"Did you now?" He felt the fierce surge of tender protectiveness that engulfed him at times like this. "We won't allow anything to harm our Bess, will we, Miss Palmer?" He patted Bess on the back and looked at the governess.

"Certainly not," she said, obviously for the child's benefit. Elinor had apparently donned her dressing gown hastily. She now belted it more firmly about her and drew it closer at the neck. Her actions made him aware of the unconfined form beneath. Turning his attention back to his daughter, he kissed Bess and lowered her to the bed.

"Go back to sleep, now, Puss," he said, touching her cheek with the back of his hand.

"Miss Palmer, too," Bess said, lifting her arms toward Elinor.

Adrian stepped back as Elinor bent over the little girl and kissed her on the forehead.

"Sleep tight, my dear," Elinor said in an audible whisper.

Bess snuggled into the covers and the two adults watched as she quickly succumbed to the innocent sleep of children. They quietly left her room. The hall was lit by a single sconce several feet away.

"Does this happen often?" he asked outside the door.

"No. Once in a while only. I heard her cry out."

She was standing very close to him. He could smell a faint trace of the scent she so often wore. He instinctively leaned a little closer, felt the warmth of her body, then caught himself. He took her hand and lifted it to his lips.

"Thank you," he said softly.

"Of course, my lord." She extricated her hand, but it

seemed to him that she did so reluctantly. For a moment it appeared she would say something else. Her eyes were deep pools of mossy green. Was that longing he saw? Regret? She turned toward her own room.

A short while later, he lay staring at the underside of the canopy over his bed, the fire across the room affording dim light. His hands were tucked behind his head, his elbows jutting out like flutterby wings.

It just does not make sense, he told himself for the thousandth time. Here was a loving, caring woman whose pronounced political views and intellectual interests so precisely paralleled his own it was uncanny. There had to be some factor he was not fitting into this equation.

That shared moment outside his daughter's room had been a revelation for the Marquis of Trenville. Whatever it was, Elinor—his Elinor—was essentially innocent. And he would use every means in his power to protect her.

Adrian was still mulling the situation over the next morning when Miss Palmer asked for a private interview with her employer.

"Yes, Miss Palmer?" He gestured for her to take a seat then leaned against his desk, his arms crossed in front of his chest and his legs crossed casually at the ankles. She remained standing.

"I regret to say that I have come to tender my resignation," she said in a formal, businesslike tone.

"Your *what?*" She had caught him completely off guard.

"My resignation. I—I find family obligations making certain demands on me."

"What sort of 'family obligations,' may I ask?" His tone was suspicious.

"An aged aunt of my father's is in serious need of a companion to aid her and I am the only one available." She twisted her hands together in front of her and refused to meet his gaze.

"I see." He stalled, knowing full well she was lying. Had he not monitored every bit of correspondence entering or leaving this house? Wait. Perhaps her visit the other day had been to a relative. "And just when did you learn of this obligation?"

"Only recently, my lord." She looked up him, her expression unreadable. "I shall, of course, stay on until you can find a replacement."

"How very generous of you. Tell me, Miss Palmer," he said biting out the name sarcastically, "have you no sense of obligation to *my* family? To children who have grown fond of you?" *To an employer who loves you,* he added silently and angrily to himself.

"Indeed I have." She seemed taken aback by his vehemence. "This decision has not been easy for me. I am extremely fond of the children and I shall miss them fiercely."

"But not enough to reconsider your apparently hasty decision to leave." He straightened, took a step toward her, and grabbed her by the shoulders. "Now—look me in the eye and tell me you truly want to leave."

She twisted away from him, refusing again to meet his intense gaze. She drew a ragged breath. "It is not a matter of 'want.' Please believe me when I tell you this is in your best interest, my lord."

"In *my* best interest? Allow me to doubt that most sincerely." Fueled by her turning away from him, his anger was barely in check now. "I would have an explanation for *that* very singular idea."

"I'm sorry. I cannot give you one."

*"Can*not? or *will* not?"

"Please. Just take my word for it. And, please, Adrian . . ." There was a distinct catch in her voice. "Please don't make this more difficult than it already is."

He was profoundly moved by her obvious distress. His anger melted into concern.

"Elinor," he said gently, "I am sure there is more to this than an aged aunt. She must have existed before you took this position. If you are in some kind of trouble, perhaps I can help."

"No!" Then her voice softened. "I mean—no, there is no trouble. I simply must leave, though."

He lifted his hands in a gesture of resignation. "Have it your way, then. I shall advertise the position immediately. I have your word you will stay until we find a replacement?"

"Of course."

"Good."

Yes, good, he thought as she left the room. *That at least gives me some time to try to solve this dilemma.* He turned the conversation over and over in his mind. He dismissed that business about an aunt.

She was resigning because it was in *his* best interest, was she? Did that mean she regretted her spying activities? She must think they would reflect on him. And *that* could only mean she cared for him. This thought came as a delightful discovery.

Are you so sure of that? What about this "Peter?" Well, whoever he was, Peter could damn well look out for himself. Adrian Whitson, Marquis of Trenville, had no intention of allowing this woman to walk out of his life without a fight. At the very least, he would know the full story.

Thirteen

The next day brought answers to some of Adrian's questions. When he returned in mid-morning from a ride in the park, he found a highly agitated Graham anxious to speak with him.

"The widow Garrison has a sister living with her." Graham paused for dramatic effect. "The sister is one Harriet E. Palmer."

Adrian's heart sank. Despite clear evidence of altered documents and testimony from the Spensers, he had hoped against hope for some reasonable explanation of *his* Miss Palmer's identity.

"Did you speak with either woman?"

"No, sir. Didn't know as yuh'd want me tippin' your hand in that regard."

"Quite right. The element of surprise may help when I visit this Miss Palmer who is, I assume, the genuine article."

That very afternoon he presented himself at lodgings let to Mrs. Garrison.

"Lord Trenville to see Miss Harriet Palmer," he announced to the manservant who responded to his knock. He heard clearly the man's repeating his announcement and a muffled yelp before a cultured female voice said, "Please show him in."

"Miss Palmer?" he asked, for there were two women in the room.

"Yes." It was apparently the older of two elderly women who responded. "This is my sister, Mrs. Garrison." She invited him to have a seat.

"Miss Harriet E. Palmer?"

"Yes. I am she."

He noted that she offered no further information, nor did she ask his business. *Not going to make this easy for me, are you?* he thought. Aloud, he said, "You were once employed by Sir Cecil Spenser, were you not?"

"Yes, I was."

Did she sound somewhat reluctant in admitting this? He decided to be blunt. "Just who is the woman who used your credentials to gain a position as governess to my children?"

"I beg your pardon?" Miss Palmer's voice was startled, but he thought he could fairly hear the wheels turning in her mind. Mrs. Garrison gave a strangled little cry.

"Miss Palmer," he said firmly, "let us not play cat-and-mouse games here. Who *is* the woman in charge of my children? She was followed to this address only a few days ago."

"I am truly sorry, my lord, but I am not at liberty to say." She *did* sound sorry, he thought, but he also noted there was no denial.

"Apparently, madam, you do not fully appreciate the gravity of the situation. You have allowed yourself to be party to deception. You may be held liable for your role in this fraud."

At this, Mrs. Garrison said weakly, "Oh, dear. Perhaps you had better tell him, sister."

"No, Lucinda. I cannot reveal a secret that is not mine to reveal."

Adrian found himself admiring the woman's loyalty even as she frustrated his efforts to learn the identity of the woman she protected.

"I understand your reluctance to break a trust," he said,

"but I have reason to believe Elinor—if that is, indeed, her name—may be in some kind of trouble. I want to help her."

Miss Palmer seemed genuinely torn. She started to say something, then changed her mind. Finally, she said, "Yes, her name is Elinor."

"That much is true, then," he said.

"Yes. Please believe me, my lord, there was never any fraud aimed at you. Elinor is an honorable lady."

"You will forgive me if I question that, will you not? People of honor do not gain employment under false pretenses." Nor do they spy for enemy powers, he might have added. He did not say this, though, for who knew how deeply involved this Miss Palmer and her sister were? His instincts told him these two were what they seemed, but he must be cautious.

"I have known her for many years, sir. She is a truly good person."

"I am inclined to agree with you despite—" Something clicked. "Many years? Was she perhaps one of your own charges then?"

Miss Palmer looked at him in alarm and put her hand to her mouth as though to keep the words in.

"That *is* it, is it not?" he demanded. "You were her governess and she turned to you for help?"

"Please, my lord. I cannot betray a confidence. You must take this up with La—with Elinor."

"All right," he said grimly, "but know this, Miss Harriet E. Palmer. If there are any legal consequences of her actions, you, too, will be prosecuted. Good day, ladies."

He arose and left the room, not waiting for the servant to show him out. He was furious at having achieved so little. Perhaps the men from Bow Street could ferret out information on the real Miss Palmer's former employers, other than the Spensers.

* * *

The morning after she informed Trenville she would be leaving, Elinor descended the stairs to breakfast still caught in an emotional storm.

Never in her life had she been so torn in her feelings. She knew full well Trenville would not welcome her resignation, but the vehemence of his objection surprised her. If he only knew the truth, she thought, he would be eager for her departure.

She had stoically dealt with his initial distrust and sarcasm. By not looking at him directly, she had thought herself safe from his penetrating gaze. But then he had become solicitous, genuinely concerned for her welfare. Only the knowledge of how much he would be hurt by the truth had kept her from throwing herself in his arms and blurting out her story.

And he would be hurt.

A scandal might well prove a nine days' wonder in social circles, but how might it play in the delicate balance of political and diplomatic circles? Beyond these considerations was a deeper level of possible hurt. His personal sense of honor was such that he would undoubtedly find her deception not only painful, but disgusting. That, she could not bear to see.

"Miss Palmer." He greeted her cordially if somewhat coolly as she entered the breakfast room.

"Good morning, sir."

"I have had the children's ponies brought to the city. They arrived yesterday."

"How wonderful. The girls and Geoffrey will be so excited."

"I thought as much." He paused. "I also had the Lady Titania brought up."

"Oh," she said in a small voice.

"I gave the order before we knew of your plan to leave." Was his tone slightly accusatory? "You may as well enjoy riding her while you are yet here."

"Thank you, my lord."

"There you go—'my lording' me again." This time, his tone was lighter and some of the customary warmth had returned to his smile.

"I'm sorry, m—Adrian. Force of habit." She smiled back at him and their gazes locked for a moment. She looked away first, but in that instant felt some of their old rapport had been reestablished.

"Uh . . . Elinor . . ."

She looked at him expectantly.

"I think there is no reason to tell the children just yet of your plan to leave. I do not want them upset."

"As you wish, Adrian."

"Time enough to tell them when the event is closer."

Elinor readily agreed, for she wanted to postpone her good-byes to the younger members of the household as long as possible.

For a few days, her life assumed its usual routine with the welcome addition of rides in the park. Often Elinor would go alone in the early mornings—alone, except for the ever-present groom who accompanied her. She noted that her companion on these rides, as well as on the rides she took with the children, was invariably the same man, one who had, she knew, joined Trenville's staff only recently. At Whitsun Abbey, their companion had always been whichever groom was free at the moment. She wondered about this, but other matters pushed it out of her mind.

As she knew they would be, the children were ecstatic about having their beloved ponies with them again. Recalling happier days when she and Peter had ridden together, Elinor enjoyed watching the pure pleasure Geoffrey, Bess, and Anne took in their riding ventures.

Leaving these little people was going to be very hard. Leaving his lordship would be even harder. Enough. She would concentrate on being happy with the time she had left. To this end, she found herself spending more of her free time with the children, indulging them more, and hugging them more often and more tightly. Sometimes it seemed her arms just did not want to relinquish those small bodies.

She longed for the comfort of Adrian's arms about her. If only she could unburden herself to him. She had occasionally seen him look at her with—what? Speculation? Regret? Longing? Then he would seem to catch himself and in the next instant his emotions would be carefully veiled.

His reaction to her resignation had gone beyond an employer's disappointment at losing a valued employee, had it not? Surely those kisses meant something to him, too.

Perhaps she should confide in him as Harriet Palmer had suggested. Why? So his overdeveloped sense of duty would compel him to help her? So his rigid sense of honor would trap him into doing something he did not want to do?

No. She simply could not put him in such a position.

Adrian was preoccupied with the private dilemma of trying to find out who Elinor really was and devising a means of postponing her departure. Then, suddenly, a monumental public issue intruded and intensified his own problems.

Canning had invited Nathan Olmstead to join his closest advisors in a morning meeting.

"Bonaparte has escaped," the Secretary said without preamble.

"What?!"

"It cannot be!"

"You heard me correctly. He fled. Managed to get off the island of Elba. Just sailed away with a small army of followers one night."

"My God."

"Now what?"

"Napoleon is on his way to Paris, apparently gathering

strength as he goes. Wellington has left Vienna to take command of the armies in Belgium."

"What about the Congress in Vienna?" Morton asked.

"And the treaty?" Dennington added.

"No treaty. The Congress has broken up, though the alliance is still more or less intact."

"So England is 'more or less' on her own again," Morton said flatly.

"More or less." Canning flashed a grim little smile. "Which brings us to our most pressing matter. It is absolutely imperative now that we apprehend this spy." He looked at Adrian who had sat quietly throughout this exchange.

"Captain Olmstead and I have a plan that might work," Adrian said slowly.

"Well, out with it, man," Morton demanded.

"Suppose we put it out that certain information is so sensitive that it can only be passed on to a special courier at an isolated location. Our man—"

"Or woman," Olmstead interjected.

"Or woman," Adrian continued just as though he had not been interrupted and just as though his heart had not skipped a beat, "will feel compelled to intercept the message."

"And can do so only at the rendezvous point." Dennington crowed in delight.

"Actually, he will probably observe the rendezvous, then follow the receiving courier," Olmstead explained. "He will be intercepted when he attempts to take the message from our man."

"Won't he suspect a trap?" Morton asked.

"Possibly," Adrian conceded. "But Napoleon needs information. Whoever it is will have to take the risk."

The meeting continued with their working out details. The spy would undoubtedly enlist the aid of some of his—or her—cohorts in trying to obtain information ostensibly destined for Wellington in Belgium. The receiving courier would be followed by the foreign agents *and,* discreetly, by the Crown's men who would move in at the point of interception.

"So, let me get this straight," Morton said. "Trenville receives a message that important information is not being handled in the usual manner. Instead, it is to be delivered to a courier at the Golden Hart Inn."

"Right," Olmstead said.

"We assume the spy will be there to see the delivery?" Morton went on.

"Won't he be afraid Trenville will recognize him?" Dennington asked.

"Yes. And that is precisely why the delivery must be made by one of you, not Trenville," Olmstead said.

"What about *you?*" Morton asked Olmstead.

"Captain Olmstead was a frequent guest at my home in Devon. Assuming this agent is someone within my household, he might be put off at seeing Olmstead show up." Adrian refused to think of the agent as a possible *she.*

"You gentlemen are all known to be privy to sensitive information and are well enough known in polite society to be readily recognized by our man," Olmstead said.

"Well, it would not make much sense for the foreign secretary to be delivering such information himself," Dennington said with a gesture toward Canning. "I volunteer."

"Here, now," Morton objected. "Why you instead of me? I volunteer as well."

"Now consider carefully, gentlemen," Adrian said. "This could prove quite dangerous."

"No more so than your little jaunts to the continent," Dennington argued. "Morton's wife is expecting to be confined shortly. You two"—he indicated Canning and Trenville—"are out of the running. I am afraid, my friends, that leaves me as your logical choice. Jonathan William Prentiss,

Viscount Dennington, at your service." He gave a smart little bow of his head and shoulders.

"That settles it, then," Canning agreed. "Thank you, Dennington. This will not go unnoticed."

"And there will be adequate protection at the inn," Olmstead assured him.

"We need to act on this immediately, gentlemen." Canning turned to Olmstead. "Captain, can we have the necessary men in place in, say, three days' time?"

"Yes, I believe so."

"Trenville? You can handle your end by then?" Canning asked.

"Yes, sir."

Adrian left the meeting with mixed feelings. At last they seemed on the verge of catching the enemy agent who had proved so elusive. But what if Elinor were involved? How could he protect her?

Well, he could not be the one at the inn, but he could certainly be on the scene later. If necessary, he would simply whisk her away.

Fourteen

Elinor could not shake the feeling that she was being watched whenever she stepped outside the confines of Trenville's town house. She told herself she was being silly. The fact that she often observed two or three men on the street with seemingly little to do was irrelevant. They were undoubtedly neighborhood servants trying to avoid or postpone unpleasant tasks.

She had listened patiently the morning after her visit to Miss Palmer as Trenville gently, but firmly dressed her down for going off alone. He explained that his government position dealt with sensitive issues and materials as she well knew and that members of his household might thus become targets for unscrupulous persons. That was, of course, why both a maid and a groom always accompanied her and the children to the park. The same precautions were to be in effect when she went out without the children. She had apologized and that had been the end of it. Still, there was this nagging feeling that the situation was not as innocuous as his lordship would have her believe.

London drawing rooms buzzed with news of Napoleon's escape from Elba and his triumphal march to Paris. Fashionable matrons, society misses, and gentlemen of the *ton* who called on the marchioness talked of little else. The women whispered fearful tales of atrocities and the "monster's" brutalities, savoring the most outlandish details. The men blustered about how the British army under Wellington would make short work of dealing with the Corsican upstart. After all, it had been done once. . . .

Listening to this venting of fears and bravado, Elinor was struck by the artificiality of it all. The real danger lay across the English Channel. These women were safe enough and, as far as she could see, delighted in their shock and fear. It was better than a scary gothic novel. As for the men— they mostly brought a suppressed little snort of disgust. Elinor knew few of these darlings of the *ton* would shed their showy coats by Weston for an army uniform. Many of them did not even bother to keep abreast of matters before Parliament, let alone take their seats in that venerable body.

One afternoon, the children having been relegated to their own quarters, Elinor joined the adult members of Trenville's household for tea in the formal drawing room. It was rather a large and motley gathering of folk, with little groups scattered here and there. Elinor was not pleased to find the fawning, socially ambitious Lady Vincent among the guests. However, she remembered the woman as a favorite of the marchioness, the two of them sharing their love of gossip.

Elinor accepted a cup of tea with a smile for the footman serving it and found herself a place on a window seat somewhat removed from the rest of the room. Soon Huntington came to stand near her. She gave him a warm greeting of welcome.

"Ah, Miss Palmer. Hiding yourself way from the rest of us, are you?" he asked teasingly. There was a speculative look in his eyes.

"Not really. Sometimes it is fun just to watch people."

"Yes, I see what you mean." His gaze followed hers to where Adrian seemed trapped by a bevy of females. "I see the tenacious Lady Gabrielle has joined her mother-in-law's efforts to find Trenville a new wife."

Elinor felt a piercing jolt of pain at this comment, but

she managed to say lightly, "He does not appear to be suffering unduly."

"But appearances can be deceiving, can they not . . . my lady?"

Elinor was startled at the sort of pregnant little pause he used before the title. Her eyes connected with Huntington's knowing look. "I—I suppose so," she said slowly, looking away and attempting to keep her tea from sloshing into the saucer while she tried to think. What did Thomas Huntington know? And what danger did he pose?

"Come now, my dear," he said edging her over to sit beside her. "You are no governess. Though why an earl's sister would pretend to be one is beyond me."

"An earl's sister?" she repeated foolishly, trying to marshall her thoughts even as the conversations and laughter in the rest of the room sounded in her ears. She took a long drink of tea and calmly asked, "What *are* you talking about?"

"Doing it too brown, Elinor—I *may* still call you Elinor, may I not?"

"I—what do you mean? How—?" Dear God. This could not be happening. Not here. Not now. She looked around, seeking an escape. She saw clusters of people laughing, talking, flirting, gossiping. For an instant, they all seemed to be talking about her, looking at *her*. She closed her eyes and quickly opened them. No. They were all fully occupied with their own concerns. She carefully set her empty cup on a small table within reach.

"It's all right. You mustn't panic," Huntington assured her with a friendly pat on her hand. "No one else knows—yet."

Elinor felt cold and numb. Her shoulders slumped. "How did you . . . ?"

"I was in the library this morning copying out some letters when a fellow came to ask whether Lady Elinor Richards was a guest here. Trenville was out, so I spoke with the man. When he said he represented the Earl of Ostwick and described her ladyship, it occurred to me that yes, indeed, we did know her."

"Have you told Ad—Lord Trenville?"

"No."

"Why not?" She was amazed that she could be so calmly curious as her careful disguise—indeed, her future—was disintegrating.

"Why? First off, I've not seen Trenville since early this morning—that is, until right now. And secondly, I was, frankly, wondering if you would be able to make it worth my while not to tell him."

"Worth your while? . . . Money? You want money?" She had not raised her voice, but there was a note of panic in it. "But that is—You? Thomas—*you* would blackmail me?"

"Such an ugly word, my dear." He patted her hand again.

This could not be happening. She looked around the room once more, shocked at how ordinary it seemed. Her gaze locked with Adrian's for a moment. She quickly looked away. Think. She had to think.

"What did you tell the man who came inquiring?" Her voice was controlled, despite the maelstrom of emotions swirling within.

"Nothing, yet. He gave me his direction, though. Seemed pretty sure you—that is, her ladyship—had been to this house. Offered a reward for information."

"I—I see. And if I 'make it worth your while' you will not tell him I am here? And you will not reveal any of this to Lord Trenville?"

He nodded. "You have the right of it. Can we come to an agreement then?" He named a sum that caused her to blanch.

She heaved a long sigh. "I will need some time. Needless to say, in my present situation, I haven't a sum like that readily available."

"I shall give you time. After all, neither of us is going

anywhere." His laugh signified the warm friendliness they had shared before, but there was a hollow ring to it and his blue eyes were hard. "Say—three days?"

She gasped.

"All right, then—four. But no more."

Elinor picked up her cup and casually made her way to the tea table, speaking and nodding to those who acknowledged her. She had to get out of this room. She had to *think*. She passed behind the settee on which Lady Vincent sat with Gabrielle, the two of them holding court, as it were. Elinor was stunned to hear her own name.

"No, my dear," the woman was saying. "They've not found Lady Elinor Richards yet. But her uncle is a determined man. Arabella is certain he will succeed."

Arabella again. Drat that woman. Elinor set her cup and saucer on a tray held by a footman and edged toward the door. She looked around the room and again caught Adrian's eye. She had to get out of here before anyone commented on the sameness of the names of a missing heiress and a governess.

That evening Adrian sent word to the children's rooms that he wished to speak with Miss Palmer. This afternoon, it had seemed to him that she was frightened or upset. He had to try one more time to break through the barrier she kept so firmly in place. The rendezvous with the spy was set for tomorrow night. Dressed to go out later to his club, Adrian waited for her in the library.

"You wanted to see me, my lord?"

She had apparently received his summons as she was preparing to retire. Her hair had been hastily piled atop her head and stray wisps sneaked out here and there. He thought removal of a pin or two would send the whole mass tumbling to her shoulders. His fingers itched to do just that.

"Yes, Miss Palmer—Elinor." He indicated a wing chair

near a small table with a lamp on it. In the soft light, her hair gleamed and her skin glowed. She nervously licked her lips and he thought how very kissable that mouth was. He took the matching chair. "I—I was wondering if you have had any second thoughts about our conversation the other day?"

"My leaving, you mean?"

"Yes."

"No, my lord. I have written Lady MacGregor explaining the situation to her."

"I see." He sat quietly for a brief moment. "My sister, Lady Tellson, is in town with her children. We have thought of planning a fireworks display for her son's birthday. Would you care to join our families for this outing?"

"Oh, yes." Her eyes lit with anticipation. "The children will love it—and so will I. When?"

He watched her carefully as he answered. "I thought perhaps tomorrow evening? Or the next?"

"Wonderful," she said without hesitation. "I shall see that the children are prepared."

"Ogilvie has a large estate on the edge of town. He has offered the use of one of his pastures. We shall return by the children's usual bedtime."

"You are not worried about a coach being attacked and robbed, traveling after dark?"

"Not with two outriders and two footmen on each coach as well as Tellson and myself. The servants can also help us keep track of overly excited children."

"That is probably a good idea, especially in view of Geoffrey's sense of adventure." She smiled indulgently, apparently recalling some incident with Geoffrey. Was it quite proper for a man to envy his son?

"Tomorrow is all right then?" he asked, again observing her carefully.

"Yes, of course, if that is your wish." She looked at him in surprise.

He shook himself mentally. Her surprise was natural—after all, his slightest whim was to be satisfied by an employee, was it not?

"Will that be all, my lord—Adrian?" She quickly added his name on seeing his eyebrow lift.

"Yes." Instead of waving her off as he would an ordinary servant, he rose and took her hand to lift her from her chair. When she stood before him, he still held her hand and she seemed in no hurry to retrieve it. "I do wish you would reconsider your decision to leave," he said softly.

"I—I wish I could do so."

She looked into his eyes and he knew it was true—she wanted to be here, with him. "Elinor—" His voice was husky as he moved his hands to her elbows to pull her closer. "Are you sure?" he whispered as his lips brushed hers.

Then he was holding her tightly, pressing his mouth firmly to hers. She entwined her arms around his head and he felt her fingers in his hair. He deepened the kiss, and with a soft moan, she allowed his tongue to probe. She responded with a fervor that threatened to push him over the edge. He pulled back slightly to shower kisses on her eyelids, her ear, trailing his lips down her neck, pushing his hands through her sweet-smelling hair.

"Are you?" he whispered at her ear.

"Am I what?"

He laughed quietly at the distracted note in her voice. "Are you sure you must leave?"

This seemed to bring her to her senses. She stiffened and stepped back; her hands pushed against his chest. He refused to release her.

"Please, Adrian," she begged, a catch in her voice. "I must."

He dropped his arms and stared into mossy green orbs that reflected his own longing and despair.

"I must," she repeated and turned to leave.

He watched her go, cursing himself for losing control. Just cannot keep your hands off her, can you, Trenville?

But his heart sang at the thought that she had so readily agreed to an outing that might take place at the very same time the spy would be trying to intercept an important message. She had not so much as flinched a muscle or fluttered an eyelash at the suggested time. She was either innocent— or the consummate actress! He did not doubt her sincere reaction to his embrace. No acting there.

Still worried, but more hopeful than he had been previously, he picked up his hat and set off for his club.

Elinor returned to her chamber, flung herself on the bed, and let the tears flow. Earlier she had taken little comfort in knowing her instincts were right in the feeling of being watched. She knew the man with whom Huntington spoke was not representing the *Earl* of Ostwick, but the young earl's guardian. Her uncle was on to her. Only Huntington's greed had given her a temporary reprieve.

Huntington. What a cad he turned out to be. Having thought of him as a friend, she was shocked and sickened to discover he would sell her out to the highest bidder. On the other hand, had he not let drop subtle hints that he enjoyed the high life? His wardrobe bespoke a man of wealth, if somewhat questionable taste. He made no secret that his social life included gambling and associating with some of society's high flyers. Thomas liked to drop the names of exalted acquaintances into his conversations. Why had it not occurred to her that he was living beyond his means?

But, then, why should it have mattered to her? Thomas's behavior was not a subject for her concern—until now. Where on earth could she hope to come up with such a sum as he demanded in only four days? Impossible. And even if she could produce it, how much would he demand the next time? Elinor Richards was not so naive as to believe a successful blackmailer would not come back for more.

She could see no other way out—she would have to break her word to Adrian and leave before he found a replacement governess. On that fourth day, when Huntington came to assert his claim, she would simply no longer be around.

As a governess, she had hoarded her wages, spending very little on "fripperies" that Lady Elinor would not have thought twice about. If she still had not heard from Mary MacGregor in three days' time, she would board a stage for the north anyway. Once there, if she were turned away, surely she could find *someplace* to hide for the few months until her birthday. She would cross that bridge when she came to it.

Meanwhile, she would savor each moment she had left with Adrian and the children. She looked forward to the promised outing. It would be her last chance to share a positive experience in their lives.

The following morning at breakfast, Adrian informed her the proposed outing was to be postponed until the *next* evening by his sister's request.

"Well, then, we should postpone mentioning it to the children," she said. "I am quite sure the prospect of viewing a fireworks display tomorrow would totally eclipse any lessons today."

Adrian chuckled. "I suppose you are right. We will tell them tomorrow. Meanwhile, you may have their undivided attention."

"I would never be so overly confident as to assume that," she said, smiling, "but I need no additional competition for their attention."

As it turned out, there were few distractions that day. Overcast weather, threatening showers, discouraged outdoor activities. The children contentedly devoted themselves to the three Rs, though Elinor thought reading and 'riting took precedence over 'rithmetic on this day.

She made a mental note to leave detailed accounts of each child's strengths and weaknesses in their various studies, since she would not be available to ease the new governess into the job. This thought saddened her, but what could she do?

Lessons finished for the day, Elinor regularly turned her charges over to the nursery help. Occasionally, she shared the children's "tea," but more often than not, she pursued some interest of her own. Sometimes that was reading; sometimes she played the pianoforte in the music room; and often she would take a long walk. At Ostwick Manor, she mused, she would be in the garden encouraging some fragile specimen to survive and produce. Governesses, however, did not usurp the Trenville gardeners' chores. So, on this day, she walked.

She was accompanied by Millie, one of the upstairs maids who was often her companion on such ventures since Trenville had decreed that she never go out alone here in the city. In truth, Elinor welcomed the girl's company. Millie chatted amiably about gossip belowstairs and about her family back home in Staffordshire.

The two had left Trenville House with Millie carrying an as yet unnecessary umbrella. They had gone about a quarter of mile, neither paying much attention to the traffic on the street, which, in any event, was not very heavy at that time of day.

"Now me younger brother is a dreamer," Millie was saying, "Mum says he musta been a changeling, but she be only teasin', o'course."

Elinor was only half listening, but murmured seemingly attentive sounds as Millie chattered on. Suddenly, the sound of a team's hooves on the cobblestones sounded very close and a carriage stopped just in front of the two young women. Elinor noted it was a plain, closed vehicle, sporting no crest, nor uniformed attendants.

The door opened and a large man jumped out, grabbed Elinor by the arm and shoved her toward the open door. Surprise and terror seized her.

"No! Stop! Let me go!" she screamed, while frantically jerking away from the iron grip on her arm.

" 'Ere, now," Millie shouted and swung her umbrella at the attacker.

The man gave Millie a hard slap, knocking her to the ground. Then, effortlessly, he lifted Elinor, shoved her into the coach, climbed in after her, and even as he closed the door, the vehicle was moving away at a fast clip. Stunned, Elinor raised herself to her knees.

"What . . . ? Who . . . ? *You!*" she shrieked.

"Now is that any way to greet a long absent relative?" her uncle asked with a self-satisfied smile on his face. "Do get off the floor, my dear. It is a most unladylike position." She ignored the hand he extended and took the seat opposite him and his henchman.

"Stop this coach immediately and let me out of here," she demanded, thinking a show of bravado might carry the day.

It didn't.

"I am sorely afraid that is not possible," Brompton said smugly. "You just relax. We will reach our destination in due time."

"Which is *where?* Where are you taking me?"

"Your bridegroom awaits."

His words came like a splash of icy water. She sucked in a deep breath and longed to smash the smirk off his face.

"If you think for even an instant that I will marry that degenerate old roué you have chosen for me, you can just jolly well think again," Elinor said through gritted teeth. "Now, stop this coach, or I will jump out as it moves."

"Burt." Brompton nudged his man who moved over to

the seat beside Elinor. "If you don't behave yourself, my dear, Burt will have to tie your hands and feet. Pity if that should be necessary. He is not a gentle fellow."

Elinor swallowed the panic that threatened to engulf her. Her immediate thought was that she had to keep her hands and legs free. There might still be opportunity for escape. Her shoulders slumped as she moved farther back in the seat.

"Good. You are beginning to see reason," her uncle said.

"I see you have the power to hold me against my will, but there is no way you can make me marry against my will."

"Oh, I think there is." Brompton's voice was deceptively soft, but carried an undercurrent of triumph and menace. "If you care about your brother at all, you will be eager to marry exactly where I tell you."

"Peter! What have you done with him? If you've harmed him . . ."

"You will do what?" he sneered. "I am calling the shots here, my dear. And unless you do exactly as I say, your brother is likely to suffer a very serious accident. This is not the way I wanted to do this, but you have given me no choice, my girl."

"Where is Peter? I want to know he is safe."

"You will see him soon enough. He will serve as an additional witness as you become the baroness, Lady Pennington, before the night is over."

Fifteen

Adrian was sitting in the library with Nathan Olmstead, going over details of the plan to catch their spy in the act, as it were.

"If our man takes the bait, I don't see how this can fail," Adrian said.

"You are sure the main culprit is a male of the species?" Olmstead's voice was even.

"Not absolutely. But I *am* sure that it is not Miss Palmer." Adrian had decided to confide this much about Elinor.

"You have proof then?"

"Not the kind that would stand up under scrutiny, but I know I am right."

Olmstead measured his words carefully. "Adrian, you are not allowing your feelings for her to cloud the issue, are you?"

"My feelings? Is it that obvious, then?"

"Only to someone who has known you since boarding school days—twenty years, more or less."

"Well, my feelings—"

At this point, they were interrupted by a clatter of noise in the hall and a hurried knock on the door which opened to reveal an agitated footman and a disheveled maid.

"She's been nabbed, sir," the footman said. Both the servants were breathing hard as though they had been running.

Adrian stood. "Get hold of yourselves. Who has been nabbed?"

"Miss Palmer's been snatched, my lord," the maid said with a sob.

Adrian felt an iron fist reach into his innards and twist hard. Fear held him for only an instant. Then the mind that had seen a naval officer through terrible battles and a diplomat through Machiavellian subtleties took over. Knowing it was important to get the details immediately, Adrian poured two glasses of sherry and handed them to the footman and maid, ignoring their surprise.

"Here, drink this. And tell me exactly what happened. Rowlands, isn't it?" he asked the male servant.

"Yes, sir. Graham and Seaton followed the coach what took her. Said Millie and me should come back and tell you what happened."

"Begin at the beginning."

Millie squared her shoulders. "Me an' Miss Palmer was jus' takin' a walk when outta nowhere this carriage . . ."

With an occasional interruption from Rowlands, she related the events of the last half hour.

Even before they were finished, Adrian issued an order to have his and Olmstead's carriages brought around and he named another servant who was to report to him immediately—with weapons. At the end of the narrative, he and Olmstead asked a few questions to refine details, then dismissed the maid.

"They saw clearly only the man who shoved her into the carriage," Olmstead said. "Big. A shock of red hair. Not much to go on."

"And another man in the coach, but Millie did not get a good look at him. She *guessed* he was Quality."

"I seen that redheaded feller somewhere," Rowlands said. "But danged if I remember where. Mebbe Graham or Seaton will know 'im."

"Graham, Seaton, and Rowlands are Bow Street Runners," Adrian explained. "And there are more. They have been helping in our investigation."

Olmstead whistled in appreciation. "Well, that should be to our advantage."

"The coach is ready, my lord," a figure at the door announced.

"Nate, I am going after Elinor." Adrian unlocked a drawer in the desk at one end of the room and took out a set of pistols. "You are on your own tonight. Can you handle it?"

"I think His Majesty's forces can muddle through," Olmstead said dryly.

"Rowlands, you come with me. I have a couple of stops, then we will be on our way after that coach."

He was lucky. Harriet Palmer was at home when Adrian pounded on her door moments later. Miss Palmer stood in the doorway of her drawing room.

"All right—who is she?" he demanded without preamble. "I have to know. Now. Elinor has been kidnapped."

"Kid—oh, my goodness." She put her hand to her throat.

"No. Don't you faint on me." Adrian reached out to steady her.

"I shall not fall victim to the vapors, young man," she said primly. "Allow me to catch my breath." She led him into the room and took a seat. He refused the one she offered him.

"Please. Just tell me what I need to know. I have to go after her."

She looked at him steadily, apparently weighing his words.

"Good heavens, woman. This is serious. You must help me."

"Yes, I think I must," she conceded.

"Well . . . ?"

"Your Elinor is Lady Elinor Richards, daughter of the tenth Earl of Ostwick. Her younger brother is the current earl."

Adrian was stunned. "A title? She is a member of the *ton?*"

"Her lineage is probably as noble as your own, my lord." Miss Palmer's voice was matter-of-fact.

"So why is she masquerading as a governess? There must be some profound reason for such behavior. And who would kidnap her?"

"I doubt not that Brompton—with his monumental debts—is behind this," Miss Palmer said. "He and that horrid old lecher, Pennington. Lady Elinor is heiress to a considerable fortune when she marries—or when she reaches the age of five and twenty." She proceeded to give him an abbreviated version of Elinor's problems since her father's death.

"Pennington. Pennington. I know that name." Adrian searched his memory. "Good grief! Pennington?!"

Miss Palmer nodded. "The two of them plan to divide her inheritance, though the money alone is not Lord Pennington's only motivation."

Adrian hadn't the heart to tell this nice old lady just how much danger her former charge was in. Stories of Pennington's depravity were rampant among certain male enclaves.

"I thank you, Miss Palmer." He strode over to her, picked up her hand, and aimed a kiss at it. "You will not be sorry you confided in me."

"Just bring her back safe." There was a catch in her voice.

"I will. I promise."

His next stop was a gentleman's club that operated on the fringes of respectability. It was frequented by people who would know Pennington well. He brushed by the doorman who was, in any event, obsequious in his welcoming such a high-toned newcomer to his establishment.

A few minutes later, Adrian was back in his carriage, having obtained the information he required in the most blatantly undiplomatic manner of his entire career. Amazing how effective an out-and-out threat could be when it came from one of the most powerful men in the realm.

He had, in fact, learned more than he wanted to know. Pennington had a hunting box about three hours out of London, though Adrian's informants doubted it had lodged genuine hunters in some decades. It was, however, a well-used trysting place for Pennington and his cronies and their ladybirds. Occasionally, there were rumors of more sinister goings-on there, debaucheries of the most reprehensible sort.

Adrian was worried, but refused to allow himself to panic. It was highly likely that Brompton, whose own resources were apparently quite limited, would avail himself of his friend's property. Adrian also trusted that Graham and Seaton were on the scene. But they were only two men—against how many?

Could not be too many, Adrian reasoned. One did not go around kidnapping ladies of the *ton* with a whole army to spread the tale later. He checked his pistols for the tenth—or twentieth—time. The waiting as the coach bumped and swayed along was interminable. He envied Rowlands and the other man, both of whom seemed to be catnapping.

Elinor. Elinor. Her name beat a silent, steady refrain as his imagination conjured all sorts of ugly images. The usually cool diplomat was gone. If those bastards had harmed her . . .

Well, one thing was clear. Her masquerade had nothing to do with French spies. But why had she not come to him for help? Surely, she knew he cared for her? And she was not precisely indifferent to him—if one could judge by her response to his kisses. An heiress. And she had been in his household for months as little more than a servant!

They had been riding well over two hours and it had long since grown dark, though a nearly full moon gave erratic light through masses of clouds. Feeling the coach slow and stop, Adrian opened the door and put his head out.

"Seaton," he said, recognizing the man who approached.

"I been waitin' for yuh, my lord. Rec'nized the team," said Seaton, who had been working in Adrian's stables for weeks now. "Thought yuh'd be along soon."

Adrian climbed down, momentarily glad to stretch his legs. "Where is she?"

"There's a fork in the road 'bout a hundred yards yonder." Seaton gestured. "Take the left an' about two miles on is a lodge—they got her there."

"How many?" Rowlands leaned out to ask.

"That big redhead, a coachman, an' one other. But about ten-fifteen minutes ago, another coach took that fork. Two men in it, I think. Couldn't tell for sure. Too dark."

"Pennington, probably," Adrian said. "Where are they holding Miss Palmer?" He could not yet think of her as Lady Elinor.

"In a downstairs room. Lit up like a palace, it is. Seem to have someone upstairs, too, though. See shadows on a window up there now an' then. Graham's on watch."

"Climb up there and direct John Coachman," Adrian ordered. "Stop before we get there—no sense announcing our arrival. Then the four of us will go in and John can follow a bit later."

"Yes, sir," said Seaton and John simultaneously.

Elinor sat at the table in a combined dining room–drawing room of what had once been a modest hunting lodge. She was cold and hungry and terrified. She drew her shawl more closely about her.

The brutish Burt had shoved her into a chair as soon as they arrived.

"Bring the lad down," Brompton growled. He stood over her.

There were awkward sounds on stairs and Peter was pushed into the room ahead of Burt. Her brother's hands were tied and there was an ugly bruise on his cheek.

"Oh, Peter, I am so sorry." She tried to rise to go to him, longing to hug him. Her uncle's fingers bit into her shoulder, forcing her back onto the chair. Peter's face was drawn with anger and frustration. A memory of him as a child of eight refusing to allow tears to come when he had been punished flashed across her mind. Only this was much more serious.

"I'm all right, Ellie. We'll get out of this. You'll see. They cannot make this work."

"That's enough outta you," Burt growled and cuffed him lightly above his ear.

"Leave him alone!" Elinor shouted.

"Take him back upstairs," her uncle ordered. When Peter was gone, he said to her, "Now you've seen him. You do as I tell you and he will survive as the eleventh Earl of Ostwick."

"And if I don't? You'll kill him? I cannot believe even you would stoop so low."

"No. Got no stomach for murder. Burt has friends on the docks. Ships' captains are always looking for extra hands, no questions asked. Some of them pay dear for pretty young fellows."

"You monster!"

"Tut, tut. No name-calling. It does not become your ladyship." He grinned malevolently. "Now you just sit tight and wait for your bridegroom to arrive." He went to the door and yelled, "Toby!"

"Aye!" a voice called.

"Bring us some wine and something to eat."

"Be right there."

A few minutes later a short, wiry fellow with thin black hair entered the room bearing a tray with a flagon of wine, several glasses, and some bread and cheese, already sliced.

"Rather simple fare, but eat up," Brompton said, helping himself. "You'll have a fancy wedding supper later, I'm sure. Here's a toast to your coming nuptials." He lifted his glass in a mock salute.

That comment nearly turned her stomach, but she reached for bread and cheese. If she did manage to escape, her first worry should not be getting a bite to eat.

Presently they heard the arrival of a carriage. A few minutes later, Pennington and another man walked into the room. Pennington was attired in clothing that might have been fashionable on a man thirty years younger. On him it merely looked ludicrous. In contrast, his companion was dressed in serviceable, sober black and carried a Bible.

"Ah, my dear, you are looking lovely—as usual." Pennington grabbed her hand and bent over it just as he might in a duchess's drawing room. She jerked her hand away and he frowned. "Didn't you explain the way things are to her?" he asked Brompton.

"She knows. She's just stubborn."

"I'll take that out of her," Pennington said with a look at Elinor that promised retribution. "This is the Reverend Mr. Porterman. He will do the honors."

"It won't be legal," Elinor said. She turned to the clergyman. "I am shocked that a man of the cloth should be party to such a travesty."

"Lord Pennington has assured me he has a special license," the reverend said. "I daresay you would be very surprised at what a clergyman can do—given the right incentive."

"Enough guineas, you mean," sneered Pennington. He pulled a paper from his pocket and laid it on the table in front of Elinor. It was the special license, signed and sealed by a bishop. "All right and tight, my love. Now, can we get this over with?"

"I need a drink first," the minister said, reaching for the wine.

"Good grief." Pennington gave out a long-suffering sigh. "That's what comes of getting a drunk to do a job."

Fascinated, they all watched the man's Adam's apple bob up and down as he swallowed. He wiped his mouth on his sleeve.

"Now—get on with it," Pennington ordered. He grabbed Elinor's arm to jerk her to her feet beside him.

"This cannot be happening," she wailed, trying to free herself from his grip. "Please . . ." Her eyes appealed first to her uncle then to the minister.

"Just do it," Pennington ordered the clergyman.

"Ah . . . dearly beloved," the minister intoned with a loud belch, "we are gathered here to join this man and this woman in holy matrimony."

"I think not," said a voice in clipped tones as the entrance door crashed open.

"Adrian!" Elinor gasped.

"I hadn't even got to that part yet," Porterman complained.

"Who are you?" Pennington challenged.

"My good man, you interrupt a family matter," Brompton said in a stuffy tone.

Adrian stepped fully into the room, backed by Rowlands and Seaton, who held drawn pistols. Brompton and Pennington paled noticeably and Elinor sucked in great gulps of air to keep from fainting.

"My niece is marrying Baron Pennington with the blessings of her guardian," Brompton said. "Now, if you will just step aside and let us proceed . . ."

"She is of age and needs no blessing," Adrian said. "But that is entirely beside the point. She cannot marry him."

"And why not?" Brompton blustered, but he kept his eye

on the men with the guns. "We have a special license. Everything is in order."

"Get *on* with it," Pennington screeched. He tightened his grip on Elinor's arm and she winced at the pain.

"Adrian, they have Peter. They—they hit him," Elinor sobbed.

A part of Adrian's mind appreciated the farcical elements of this situation, even as he recognized the potential tragedy. Stall. He had to keep them from proceeding in this charade of a marriage and he had to distract them while Graham and Davies checked out what was going on upstairs and neutralized any danger there.

"Let her go," Adrian demanded.

"The woman is going to be my wife," Pennington said in an emotional frenzy.

"No, she is *not*," Adrian said. "Even if you were not deterred by my friends and their pistols, I could not let you continue. She is already married—to me."

"Adrian!" Elinor gasped. "No. You cannot . . ." Finally, she jerked free of Pennington who had relaxed his hold at Adrian's stunning announcement.

Adrian held her close but to one side of him. He nuzzled her hair even as he kept an eye on her uncle and her would-be husband. "I know we agreed to keep it a secret, my dear, but what choice do I have?" His words were clearly meant for their stupefied audience.

"I need a drink," the minister said.

"You don't understand." Elinor's tone was fierce. "They have Peter."

Peter. She was willing to go through with this for Peter? Marriage to the likes of Pennington? Well, he was damned if *he* would allow such sacrifice, no matter what the outcome for him personally. But that would have to be sorted out later.

There was noise of thumping boots and overturned furniture overhead, then of more than one person descending the stairs.

"They have Peter!" There was hysterical desperation in her voice now.

"No, they don't, Ellie. Not anymore."

A young man entered the room followed by a redheaded giant and a smaller fellow, prodded with pistols held by Davies and Graham.

"Oh, Peter. Peter." Elinor ran to him and enfolded him in her arms.

Taller than she was, Peter laid his cheek against her head, his shock of chestnut hair blending exactly with her own as she sobbed into his shoulder. "It's all right, Ellie. I'm all right. Didn't I tell you they couldn't make it work? 'Course, we had help." He raised his head and looked at Adrian, Graham, and the others. "I do thank you gentlemen."

Good God, Adrian thought, *he is no more than fifteen!* Then it hit him. Peter was Peter Richards, new Earl of Ostwick. Her brother. He had spent all this time agonizing over her love for her *brother?*

"I don't believe it," Brompton said. "If she were married to such a high-ranking member of the *ton,* we'd have heard about it. We are family."

"Are you calling me a liar?" Adrian's voice was dangerously soft.

"Good God, Brompton," Pennington warned. "Don't be a bigger fool than you already are. The man's said to be a crack shot."

"But why ain't we heard about this so-called marriage before this? We are her family," Brompton whined to the room in general, avoiding looking at Adrian. "Peter, my boy, did you know it and not tell me?"

Peter, having disengaged himself from Elinor's embrace,

still stood next to her. He looked to her for direction before responding. She shook her head.

"No. I did not know. But I would trust her judgment in such matters much more than yours. Your concern for 'family' comes rather later, Uncle."

"Why you . . ." Brompton took a step toward Peter, then abruptly stopped as Rowlands trained his pistol more directly on him.

"Don't even think about it," Rowlands warned. Then he turned to Adrian. "What do you want we should do with these fellers, my lord?"

"What I *want* would be both inhumane and illegal," Adrian said.

"These two," Rowlands indicated a man named Toby and Burt, "are in a heap of trouble already. Told yuh I rec'nized Burt here."

"Robbery, burglary—and they are connected somehow with at least two dead bodies found in the dock areas," Graham explained. "At the very least, they'll be transported. But they'll probably be hanged."

"Good," Adrian said vehemently. "Rowlands, you and Seaton take those two in and do whatever you would with them. Keep the Richards name out of your report, if you will."

"Consider it done, my lord," Rowlands said. Others in the room watched as Burt's and Toby's hands were tied behind them and they were unceremoniously ushered from the room.

"Keep your eye on these two, Graham," Adrian ordered, indicating Brompton and Pennington. "Davies, see if you can find some paper and writing instruments." Then he turned to Elinor and her brother. "Come, my dear. You and Peter have a seat over here. This will not take long and we will be on our way."

He led them to a settee at the other end of the room. Elinor had not said a word since learning her brother was safe. Adrian worried about the strain he saw plainly on her face. He wanted to hold her, tell it was all over, that he would take care of her. But she still clung to Peter.

He returned his attention to Brompton and Pennington as Davies came back with paper, ink, and two pens.

"You two sit and write what I tell you," Adrian said. When it was done, he picked up the papers, ensured the ink was sufficiently dry, folded them, and put them in his pocket. He leaned over the table and spoke softly but precisely to each of them. Then he said, "All right. Graham, you and Davies take these two back to town. Stop by Trenville House and get some more help. Then see that Lord Pennington is escorted to his estate in the north. Take Brompton to Ostwick House and put a guard on the place. Ostwick and his sister will be my guests for a day or two."

"Yes, sir."

It was nearly midnight and the strain of the last several hours had taken its toll as Elinor tried to make sense of what had happened. Adrian's announcement that she was his wife troubled her most. Why had he done that? Surely there was another way. This would surely be the principal topic in every *ton* drawing room tomorrow. Even if Brompton's tongue could be controlled, there would be no controlling his wife—or her friends.

She sat in the forward-looking seat of the coach with Peter at her side. She still clung to his hand to reassure herself she had brought no harm to her brother. Adrian sat opposite them and spoke in a matter-of-fact tone, ostensibly to Peter, but with frequent glances at Elinor for her understanding and concurrence. Elinor knew Peter was flattered to be consulted as an equal by such an out-and-outer as the Marquis of Trenville. She could only be grateful for such consideration of the younger man.

"The confessions those two signed should safely remove

them from being any further source of annoyance to either of you," Adrian said.

Curious, Peter asked, "What will happen to them?"

"Pennington has been informed that if he so much as steps off his estate within the next three years, I shall bring charges against him, and he, too, will likely be transported then, along with Burt and Toby."

"Very good, sir."

"And—and Uncle Brompton?" Elinor's voice still showed strain, but she could feel herself at last beginning to relax.

A small lantern in the coach gave off faint light. She saw Adrian's expression harden.

"Tomorrow my man of business will buy up his debts. He and his wife will be on the first ship to the Americas. If he returns, he must be prepared to repay me—or face debtors' prison. That is, unless you object . . ."

"No—" Elinor said.

"Absolutely not." Peter's voice was mature and determined.

"Our war with the United States is over. They will survive nicely if they exercise good judgment," Adrian said, reassuringly.

Exhausted, Elinor had started to doze fitfully, her head resting on her brother's shoulder, when Peter's question caught her attention.

"How did you happen on this scene so quickly, sir? And with Bow Street Runners in tow?"

She straightened, alert now. "Bow Street Runners?" How had she missed that?

"Those fellows he sent off with Uncle Brompton and the others. Really, Ellie . . ." The impatient younger brother was back.

"My lord?" She looked inquiringly at Adrian and he shifted uncomfortably.

"The men have been guarding my children, and members

of my household, ever since we returned to London and we knew a French spy was—or is—directly connected to me."

"Who?" Elinor could not hide her shock.

"We do not yet know." Adrian again shifted slightly under her gaze.

Elinor stared at him, remembering the feeling of being watched. It had been Seaton who always accompanied her and the children on their rides. And hadn't Adrian been overly fastidious about her never leaving the house unaccompanied?

"Me? You suspected me?"

"Not lately," he said. "And certainly not now."

"But you did. Adrian, how could you think that I—I—a spy? How could you? How dare you?" Utterly devastated he would think her capable of such perfidy, she stared at him in disbelief and anger for a moment, then turned her head to the darkened coach window to hide her tears.

"Elinor, please." He sat forward and tried to take her hand, but she pulled away from him. "Please. Try to understand. Elinor . . ."

Ignoring the pleading note in his voice, she turned with a stifled sob and snuggled closer to her brother. Peter put his arm around her shoulder and patted it clumsily. She was sure Peter had not missed her and Adrian's use of each other's Christian names.

She was vaguely aware of Adrian's voice explaining to Peter about the discovery of spy activities within his own household and attempts to catch such agents. Eventually, his voice trailed off as she refused to look at him.

The rest of the journey passed in silence. When they arrived at his town house, Adrian exited first and reached an assisting hand to her. She wanted to ignore it, but dared not do so lest she stumble and fall. He gave her hand a reassuring squeeze and she felt the surge of warmth his touch always brought. But this time it was accompanied by a sense of betrayal.

In the entrance hall, she started to mumble a hasty good night when she noted with some surprise Captain Olmstead emerge from the library.

Then Adrian spoke directly to her. "My lady, I believe you should hear Captain Olmstead's report."

"If you insist. Allow me to freshen up a bit and I shall be right back." She proceeded up the stairs.

Sixteen

Adrian watched as Elinor climbed the stairs, her curiosity obviously warring with fatigue and disillusionment. He wanted to take her in his arms and make her listen to him, but duty—in the person of Nathan Olmstead—once again asserted itself.

"I see *your* venture was successful," Olmstead said with a questioning glance at Peter once the library door was closed. "You brought Miss Palmer home safe and sound."

Adrian heaved a sigh. "She is not Miss Palmer. Allow me to present Peter Richards, Earl of Ostwick. She is his sister."

"A lady? You've had a lady of the *ton* acting as governess to your brats?" Olmstead gave a bark of laughter, then sobered. "She had nothing to do with this spy business then?"

"Nothing at all. Did I not say that earlier?" Adrian went to a sideboard, hesitated a moment, then poured three glasses of brandy and smiled inwardly as Peter accepted his in a grown-up manner, but succumbed to a fit of coughing with his first sip. "It goes down easier when you are more used to it," he told the boy. Then he gave Olmstead a brief summary of the chase and its outcome.

"So, the uncle—Brompton, is it?—watched the home of the former governess and traced Miss Palmer, that is, Lady Elinor, here?" Olmstead asked.

"Seems so," Adrian replied.

At this point Elinor entered the room, somewhat hesitantly. The men stood as she quietly took a seat near Peter.

She had taken time to remove her pelisse and bonnet, wash her hands and face, and recomb her hair—and felt infinitely more presentable for having done so. She thought Adrian's eyes softened with warmth when she came in and she was momentarily flustered. *Don't be silly,* she admonished herself. He thought you were a spy, a traitor.

Adrian shifted his gaze to his military friend. "All right, Nate, tell us about *your* adventurous evening."

"It went like clockwork. Exactly as we planned. Dennington met our courier, handed over the documents, and wished him Godspeed. Then Dennington left; actually, he circled around to join us as we followed the rotters who were following the courier."

"How many were there?" Adrian interrupted.

"Three. They followed our man for two or three miles at some distance, apparently trying to insure it was not a trap. Finally, they closed in on him and demanded his dispatch case. At that point, *we* closed in on *them*. There were some shots and one of them suffered a slight wound on his shoulder. I am convinced their intent was to kill the courier once he had turned over the dispatch case."

"What happened when they knew it was a trap?"

"They split up, taking off in three different directions, but luckily, there were enough of us to split up also and give chase."

"You caught them, I take it."

"We apprehended two of them."

"And the third escaped?" Adrian was clearly dismayed.

"Not exactly." Olmstead grinned. "The third agent probably *thought* the escape was successful, but in fact, we followed the third one—discreetly, of course."

"Of course," Adrian said dryly. "Followed where?"

"Here. Even as we speak, our spy is abovestairs, presumably sleeping."

"You are sure?"

"The house has been watched, front and back, since we arrived on the heels of our culprit. And there is a guard in the hallway, watching the chamber door. I thought, after all this time and trouble, you would like to be in on the actual capture." Olmstead rose and went to Adrian's desk where he had apparently been writing when Trenville and his companions returned. He handed Adrian a slip of paper. "There's the name of your spy."

Adrian raised an eyebrow in mild surprise. "I see." He went to the door and said to a footman in the hall, "Please rouse Mr. Huntington. Tell him I wish him to take some dictation on an urgent matter immediately." He gave the servant some additional instructions which the others did not hear and returned to his seat.

Elinor and her brother had sat quietly throughout this exchange. Peter seemed confused, but obviously thrilled that the other men thought to include him in such business. Elinor frankly wondered what was going on— and she was not so shy as her brother in speaking up.

"Pardon me, gentlemen, but should you not be about the Crown's business of apprehending your spy?" Still hurt that they had once thought *her* to be that spy, she could not quite control her impatience.

"In due time, my lady. In due time," Adrian said.

"I am quite sure that my presence will be superfluous as you dictate your report. With your permission, I should like to retire." She rose.

"No. Please stay. I want you to hear this. Humor me, if you will. We may be able to put some of your own questions to rest." Adrian was, she felt, making a sincere personal appeal to her. She sat back down.

A few minutes later, Huntington arrived, dressed in cotton trousers with a dressing gown tied over them. His eyes

were puffy with sleep and he was still combing his hair
with his fingers as he came through the door. His gaze took
in the presence of Olmstead and Elinor with a small show
of surprise and passed over Peter as someone unknown to
him.

His eyes came back to Elinor and she thought there was
a flicker of fear in his expression, but his voice was confident in greeting them. "Miss Palmer. We have an appoint-
ment later, I believe. Olmstead. Trenville." He nodded at
Peter.

Elinor held his gaze for a moment, then shrugged her
shoulders and shifted her own gaze to Adrian.

Adrian had stood when Huntington entered. He now drew
out a straight-backed chair near a small writing table that
faced the others at an angle.

"Sit here, Thomas. There is paper and pen handy. Ink,
as well."

"Must be truly urgent to get a fellow out of bed at such
an unconscionable hour," Huntington sounded a bit testy.

"It is very important," Adrian agreed affably. "Espionage
is always urgent."

"Espionage?" Huntington looked up in surprise. "You
have something new on those spies then?"

"We think so. Now, this memorandum is to be addressed
to Lord Canning in the usual manner. Sir"—Adrian began
to dictate, pacing about the room as he talked—"Olmstead,
feel free to correct me if I get any of this wrong."

Elinor glanced at Captain Olmstead and found him to be
watching Huntington intensely as Adrian began recounting
for the foreign secretary the events of the evening as Olmstead had related them earlier.

"And so, His Majesty's Forces managed to apprehend
two of the culprits." Adrian paused in his dictation as Huntington tried to keep up. Elinor thought Thomas looked decidedly pale. "Unfortunately," Adrian continued, "the third

escaped immediate capture." Huntington seemed to let out a long held breath very softly.

"However," Adrian went on in the dictating tone, "the third person, who turns out to have been the particular agent most responsible for our leaks, was followed . . . Sorry, Thomas. Am I speaking too fast?"

"Uh, no sir. Just let me finish . . . 'was followed.' Was he—or she—identified, my lord?"

"Yes, Thomas." Adrian's voice now carried a tone of such infinite sadness that Elinor wanted to comfort him despite her anger at him for suspecting *her* earlier. "Yes, he was. You were. It is finished."

Huntington carefully laid down the pen. He looked from Trenville to Olmstead and appeared to realize escape now was impossible. He clutched his hands between his knees. Others in the room seemed to be holding their breath, waiting for him to speak.

"It *was* a trap, then, that message tonight? I thought as much. . . ." Huntington spoke in a quiet voice of utter defeat. "And this memorandum was another trap."

"Yes. We suspected information on Wellington's troop strength would be irresistible," Olmstead said.

"Why, Thomas? Why?" Adrian sat down opposite Huntington and looked at him directly. "You had a good position. Your expectations were promising."

"Not *mine. Yours,*" Huntington said bitterly. "I have lived in your shadow far too long, Trenville. Why? Money, of course. French money allows me to live as I please—not as I must as a glorified servant."

"I expect you will be setting your sights considerably lower in Newgate," Olmstead said with little sympathy. "When I think of how many British soldiers might have died for your greed, I've a good mind to run you through myself."

Huntington turned to look at Olmstead and his eye fell on Elinor.

"Her. She told you about me, didn't she? That's how you came to suspect me. Trying to save her own skin. She is not what she seems, you know, your precious Elinor. Think I don't know what's going on between the two of you? It was *planned* that way, Trenville. She is one of us—suckered you in just as she was supposed to."

Elinor gasped. "Thomas! How could you? Blackmail could not work, so you seek to dishonor me anyway? What can you possibly gain by it?"

"I will not go down alone," Huntington sneered. "You were in on it—you go with me."

"Hear now. You can't talk to my sister that way!" Peter rose to advance on Huntington, but Elinor grabbed his wrist and Adrian waved him back to his seat.

"Oh, you won't go alone," Olmstead promised. "Those two with you tonight will be there. And there are a couple of rounders in Devonshire that have much to answer for."

"It won't wash, Thomas," Adrian said. He turned to Elinor. "He tried to blackmail you?"

She nodded.

"Well, that is over, too," Adrian said grimly. "You'll be tried for treason, Thomas. And if Lady Elinor Richards's name is even breathed in that connection, you will pay dearly."

"Hah!" Huntington's mouth twisted in an ugly sneer. "Treason. What more can you do?"

"Well," Adrian said thoughtfully, "we could arrange for you to 'escape.' Dump you in the laps of your French friends and inform them you have been playing a double game. They would not be likely to take kindly to that."

Huntington blanched and his shoulders slumped in defeat.

"Nate, take him upstairs to get properly dressed, then get him out of here. Parsons is just outside the door. He will go with you. Watch for any tricks. He may have a weapon."

"We can handle it. Browning is still upstairs and others are outside," Olmstead said. "Come along, Huntington."

Elinor watched with mixed feelings as Thomas Huntington was led from the room. Yes, he had attempted to blackmail her, had forced her into planning to break her word about staying until Trenville found a new governess. But he had been a friend in Devonshire where they had shared morning rides and achieved a degree of understanding born of their similar stations in a nobleman's household.

She had no doubt he would have carried out his threat to sell information about her to her uncle. She could not condone or forgive such despicable behavior, but she thought she understood the envy and frustration that motivated it. A firmer, more honorable character would not have succumbed to the temptation. Huntington had—and would pay a terrible price for his ambitious greed.

A year ago such thinking would not have occurred to her. So perhaps some good—some better understanding of others—had come of her masquerade.

"Ellie, are you all right?" Peter broke into her musings.

"Yes, Peter. I *am* saddened, however. Such a waste. He might have been a good man under different circumstances."

"There but for the grace of God . . . is that what you have in mind?" Adrian asked, moving to take a seat nearer the other two.

"Yes. I suppose so." Elinor was again reminded of how remarkably alike she and Adrian often thought. "Was it necessary to put him through that?" She gestured toward the writing table where Huntington had sat.

"I thought so. It was imperative that he recognize and admit his culpability. It is, of course, impossible to measure the damage he did."

"And you really suspected me?" She spoke softly, but even she could hear the pain in her voice. She searched his eyes for some ultimate truth in his response.

There was answering pain in his own gaze. "Yes. God help me—I did, though every fiber of my being cried out against it."

"Why?"

"Why did I suspect you? Or why did I not want to?"

"What made you believe I could do such a thing? I must know."

"I could not believe it. And that was a problem. The unknown French agent was someone connected to me— someone with intelligence and access, whose activities coincided with your arrival in my household. Then I met the Spensers in Belgium and learned that *my* Miss Palmer was not *their* Miss Palmer."

"Ohhh."

"But I still did not know who you were. The Bow Street Runners led me to *your* Miss Palmer, but she refused to help me—until I told her you had been kidnapped."

"She *is* a dear friend."

"I suspect she grants such loyalty only to people who have truly earned it." Adrian's eyes locked with hers for a long moment and she felt all her resentment melting away.

"See, Ellie? I warned you against going off on one of your harebrained schemes." Peter's tone was the superior tone of a young, assertive male.

"I admit I did not think it through adequately, but would you rather I had given you Pennington as a brother-in-law?"

"Good lord, no! But what are we to do now? You are not five and twenty for another six months yet. And I won't reach my majority for *years!*" His last words ended on a wail and there was silence in the room for a moment. Then Peter spoke again. "Oh, I say, that bit about you being married wasn't true, was it?"

"No!" Elinor said vehemently. "And you are not to mention it again, Peter. *That* is not to become fodder for the *ton's* gossipy cows."

Peter shrugged. "Don't know how you'll stop them once

Aunt Josephine and Lady Hempton get hold of it," he declared with the brutal honesty of youth. "Pennington ain't likely to keep quiet either."

Elinor looked in alarm first at Peter, then at Adrian, then back to Peter. She recognized the truth of Peter's statement, which merely verbalized her own fear for Adrian. Well, with her in the north with Mary MacGregor or on the Continent with her godmother, the gossip should die down soon enough.

"Why don't we discuss this in the morning?" Adrian suggested. "That is, later *this* morning?"

"That is a good idea," Elinor said. "Surely we can come up with some plausible bone to throw those dogs of gossip." As she rose and started for the door, Peter and Adrian stood as well.

"Ostwick," Adrian said, "I should like a private word with you before you go up." Elinor looked at Adrian questioningly, but he merely put his hand gently on her back to propel her toward the door. He leaned near her ear and said softly, "It is all right, my dear. Your brother is safe with me."

She gave him an uncertain smile, nearly undone by his use of the endearment and his warm breath on her ear and neck.

"Sleep well," he whispered.

"Good night, Ellie," Peter called.

Sleep well, indeed! She doubted she would get a wink of sleep, what with all the worries she had.

In the event, however, she was asleep nearly the moment her head touched the pillow.

Seventeen

Although she had fallen asleep immediately, Elinor arose early the next morning none too rested. She donned one of her serviceable "governess" dresses and said a silent prayer of thanks that she would soon have access to her own full wardrobe. Feeling nervous and uncertain of herself, she made her way to the breakfast room. She was not surprised to find Adrian there before her, but she had not expected her brother to be there as well. Judging by his near-empty plate, he had been there some time.

"Good morning, gentlemen." She gestured for them to remain seated and leaned over her brother to kiss him on the cheek before turning her attention to the food on the sideboard. She noted Peter's blush as he and Adrian returned her greeting.

"We have just been discussing details of restoring Peter's authority in his own domain," Adrian said. Elinor noted the intimacy between the two men signaled by the casual use of her brother's given name.

"Trenville is taking me to see his—and our—solicitors this morning," Peter explained. "Adrian says there should be no problem, given his actions, in having Uncle Brompton declared incompetent to act as my guardian any longer."

"Adrian," was it? She noted with amused approval the hero worship in her brother's eyes when he regarded Lord

Trenville. Peter had been too long without responsible, caring male guidance.

"You are still underage, Peter," she pointed out as gently as she could. "Someone will have to assume guardianship. I would do so, but . . ."

"But you are a female," Peter interjected.

"Yes. And everyone knows what incompetent, feather-brained dolts females are," she said, unable to hide her bitterness. "Have you and his lordship come up with a replacement, then?"

"Of course," Adrian said smoothly. "Me. With your approval, that is."

"The first thing I intend to do is discharge those villains Uncle Brompton foisted on us and bring our old servants back to Ostwick Manor and the house here in London," her brother said. "And I shall have to take a firmer hand in the management of my own estates."

At this positively mature announcement, she looked at Adrian and they shared a moment of understanding amusement. Then the true import of what Peter was saying came to her.

"I see," she said tartly. "And have you and his lordship made any other decisions about Richards family business you might deign to share with me?"

Peter looked uncomfortable and squirmed in his chair. "Ellie, it ain't like that. He was just helping me sort things out."

The eagerness had gone out of his voice and he cast an appealing glance at Adrian. Elinor was immediately sorry for taking the air from his sails. She put her plate down in the place next to him, sat down, and patted his hand.

"It's all right, Peter. I'm sure Lord Trenville has your best interests in mind."

"You are, of course, welcome to accompany us, my lady," Adrian said.

Before she could frame a reply, Gabrielle made an unprecedented appearance at the breakfast table. She swept into the room with a swish of petticoats, followed by the ever-present Madame Giroux.

"Adrian! Is it true? The servants are all abuzz. Miss Palmer is a titled lady? And poor Thomas has been arrested as a spy? It cannot be!"

"So much for any thought of slowing the dissemination of this hot topic." Adrian's tone was soft and ironic. "Yes, Gabrielle. May I introduce the Earl of Ostwick? You know his sister, Lady Elinor Richards."

There was some confusion as the marchioness and her companion were made known to the young earl and they gushed over the news of Elinor's elevation. Then they filled their plates and took seats at the table with Gabrielle talking nonstop.

"I always knew you were above the ordinary as a governess," said the marchioness who knew little and cared less about her child's lessons. "Just wait until Lady Vincent hears this news! You *will* join me as I receive callers this morning, will you not, my lady?" She turned a brilliant smile on Elinor.

"I—I think not, my lady," Elinor said with a pleading look at Adrian. "The children have their lessons, after all, and . . . and there many other matters at hand."

"Ohhh." Gabrielle pushed her lower lip out in a becoming pout. "Well, then, Adrian, she simply must accompany us to the Sheltons' ball. They will be glad to honor my request for an invitation, and we can surely find you a suitable gown." She switched her attention from Elinor to Adrian and back to Elinor.

Although she felt slightly overwhelmed by this torrent of goodwill from a woman who had scarcely noticed her before, Elinor did not give Adrian a chance to reply. "I am sorry, my lady," she said in a firm voice, "but I am not yet prepared to go on display for the *ton*. I shall, of course, be leaving this household very shortly." She rose and addressed her brother and Trenville. "No. It will not be nec-

essary for me to accompany the two of you. Please inform
Mr. Bascomb that I shall expect my usual allowance to re-
sume. My brother and I will remove to Ostwick House
when the Bromptons are gone. Now, if you will excuse me,
I have lessons to supervise."

Adrian stood. "Miss Palmer—uh, I mean Lady Elinor—"

She paused at the door and looked at him questioningly.

"You have not forgotten, have you, that there is an outing
scheduled for the children this evening? You will still accompany us, will you not? You and Peter?"

"The fireworks display. Yes, I suppose so . . ." she said
slowly.

"Fireworks!" Peter's eyes shone at the prospect—then he
apparently decided it was not quite in keeping with his new
adult status to show such enthusiasm. "That should be quite
interesting," he added in a more sedate tone.

Elinor smiled at Peter and left the room warmed by the
thought of Adrian's insistence that she join the evening's outing.

In the early afternoon when lessons were over, Elinor
ascertained that Trenville and her brother had not returned
yet. She politely refused an invitation to take tea later with
the marchioness and her guests. Instead, she called upon
Millie to accompany her to visit the modiste once patron-
ized by the fashionable Lady Elinor Richards. Surely,
Mademoiselle Violetta would have something made up that
could be quickly altered.

Elinor was determined to present herself at her very best
tonight, for this would be her farewell to Adrian and the
children. Tomorrow she and Peter would remove to their
own home and, as soon as possible, Lady Elinor Richards
would be on her way to rejoin her godmother in Italy.

She was in luck. Mademoiselle Violetta had on hand a
wonderful apricot concoction with a matching cloak. The

modiste had fashioned the outfit for a certain member of the *demimonde* who, having lost favor with her protector, failed to pick up the dress. With the addition of some ecru lace at the dangerously low neckline and a few tucks here and there it was perfect for Lady Elinor.

Spying some silk ribbon of the same apricot color, Elinor snapped it up for her hair. If this were going to be her swan song, she would most assuredly look like a swan—not the ugly duckling she had been for months now. And she would leave off those dratted spectacles, too!

"Oh, miss—I mean, my lady," Millie said that evening as she finished helping Elinor arrange her hair, "you do look most splendid."

"Amazing, is it not, what a new dress and a different hairstyle can do for a woman's looks? Not to mention her spirits!" Elinor preened in front of the looking glass. When had she ever felt so confident of her appearance? Would Adrian appreciate the transformation?

Later, as she descended the stairs, she thought he seemed to. There was definitely an approving gleam in his eyes as he stood below with Peter and the three children, waiting for her to join them.

"Ooh, Mith Palmer! You look like a printheth," Bess said in high-pitched excitement, her words whistling through a front tooth she had lost in the last month.

"She is not Miss Palmer," Anne said firmly. "You heard nurse tell us to address her as 'Lady Elinor' now."

" 'Lady El'nor'? Issat the truf?" Bess wanted confirmation from an adult.

"Yes, darling, it is." Elinor reached the bottom of the stairs and caressed Bess's cheek. "But you may call me Miss Palmer as long as you like."

Peter eyed his sister up and down with a teasingly dubious look, then nodded his approval. "I must say you look better in this outfit than in that rag you had on yesterday—or in *my* clothes the last time I saw you."

"Peter!" She gave him a quelling look and glanced at Adrian whose grin seemed to mirror her brother's.

"Come, my lady. We should be off." Adrian held her cloak and it seemed to her that his hands lingered momentarily on her shoulders before all of them were out the door and in the carriage, "ladies" on one side and gentlemen on the other.

Every time Elinor looked at Adrian, she was aware of his eyes on her. She wanted to allow herself to drown in his approving gaze, but that would definitely be unseemly with her brother and the children present. Once, she looked from Adrian to Peter and found the latter with a huge grin on his face.

"What is that you find so amusing?" she asked, smiling despite herself.

"Nothing," Peter said airily. But he did not stop grinning at her.

The three children chattered excitedly and seemed thoroughly at ease with Peter whom they had, of course, only met that afternoon.

Arriving at the Ogilvie estate, Elinor was surprised—and alarmed—to find a large number of people there, besides children and young people whom she had expected to see.

"My sister never does anything in a small way," Adrian said softly as he handed Elinor from the carriage. "There are probably twenty families here."

"And all of them members of the *ton*," Elinor said with dismay.

Indeed, it was a lavish party for a young man about Peter's age. Lady Tellson had arranged to have two large tents erected—one for an elaborate buffet supper and the other open on one side and set as a sort of gallery from which the guests would view the fireworks.

Elinor was decidedly nervous. She knew from Millie's chatter that distorted tales of her adventure and revelation of her identity would have spread like wildfire throughout London society. How would these people accept her?

"Courage, my dear," Adrian murmured. He took her hand, put it on his arm, and held it firmly to his side. As usual, his touch was both reassuring and disquieting. He steered her and his group toward his sister, the hostess of this casual party, who was conversing happily with others as they approached.

Lady Tellson turned and her group all stopped talking at once to stare at Elinor on Trenville's arm. When Elinor would have removed her hand, he refused to allow the separation.

"Caroline," Adrian said. "You have met Lady Elinor Richards. And this is her brother, Peter, Earl of Ostwick. I think you know my other companions." He gestured toward the children.

Caroline, Lady Tellson, paused and looked at her brother holding so tightly to the woman he was presenting. As she searched his eyes for a moment, Elinor recognized the concern of a sister for a brother she loved. Then a smile lit Caroline's face.

"Of course. Though I did not know you as *Lady* Elinor, now did I? Welcome, my lady. And you, my lord," she said to Peter, extending her hand to both of them and giving Elinor's a small squeeze. "May I present some of my other guests?"

With Lady Tellson's greeting setting the tone from the outset, Elinor was welcomed and marveled over in a positive way throughout the evening. One or two who had known her previously made a point of seeking her out. Elinor began to breathe more easily.

Adrian never left her side. Peter happened on some boys from his school, including the guest of honor, and the children were soon frolicking with cousins and friends, but Adrian stayed close to Elinor. When she occasionally had cause to remove her hand from his arm, it was he who always returned it to where it "belonged."

Her mind was in a whirl. He must know what this public partiality would be signaling to the other guests. Such behavior—on top of the gossip disseminated this day—could prove very harmful to a marquis, heir to a dukedom, a man who hoped to achieve great things for his country. She should separate herself from him, let others see that there was no substance to the gossip. But she could not bring herself to do so. This was perhaps the last time she would be able to enjoy his company—and it would have to last a lifetime. In a few days, she would be gone.

During the fireworks display, Adrian steered her into a chair next to his, with Geoffrey and Peter on the other side of him and Bess and Anne flanking Elinor. Soon Geoffrey was standing between his father's legs oohing and aahing at the flashes in the sky. It was not long before Bess squirmed her little body onto Elinor's lap.

"Bess!" Anne hissed. "You'll wrinkle her dress!"

"Never mind, Anne," Elinor said. "Why don't you move over here?" She extended her arm to invite Anne to take Bess's seat.

When she did so, Elinor put one arm around Anne and hugged Bess with the other. She felt such a rush of affection for these two little girls that she felt tears welling. At a sound from Geoffrey, she looked at him, then at his father. Adrian gave her a smile and squeezed her shoulder gently. He seemed to know exactly what she was feeling.

Adrian tried, without success, to maneuver Elinor into sitting beside him on the journey home. The children seemed to sense some change in these favorite adults—and as children will, they found change disquieting, fearful. They held onto what they knew. Thus it was that the Marquis of Trenville was forced to accept Elinor's sitting on one side, clutching two sleepy little girls to her, with himself on the other with his son and Peter.

When they arrived at Trenville's town house, Peter offered to carry Bess up to the nursery as Adrian carried a sleeping Geoffrey.

"No! Miss Palmer," Bess cried and wound her arms tightly around Elinor's neck.

"It's all right, Peter. Come along, Anne, dear." Elinor and Adrian shuffled the exhausted children off to the nursery, bidding Peter good night along the way.

When the children had been deposited in their rooms, Adrian found himself in the hallway with Elinor—alone with her at last.

"Will you join me in the library for a glass of wine, my lady?" he asked rather formally.

"I should like that very much. Will you give me a moment? I need to shed this cloak." She turned toward her room, then turned back to him. "Oh, and, Adrian, 'Elinor' is still just fine with me."

She flashed him a brilliant smile, but he thought there was a touch of sadness in it. He wanted to pull her into his arms here and now, but forced himself to walk calmly down to the library.

When she entered a few minutes later, he drew in a sharp breath. She had to be the most desirable woman he had ever beheld. Suddenly he felt all tongue-tied. He knew very well what he wanted to say to her, but how to get the words out?

He latched onto something inane. "I notice you have given up your spectacles." He steered her toward a settee.

"Yes." She looked embarrassed. "I—they were a part of my disguise. I thought they would make me look more like a governess."

He chuckled. "A mask to hide behind?"

"Precisely. Did it work?"

He did not answer immediately. He busied himself pouring the wine and handing her a glass before taking his own and joining her on the settee. He raised his glass in a silent salute which she answered, looking over the rim of her glass into his eyes.

"Did it work?" he repeated foolishly. "For others, perhaps, but I have never found it easy to think of you as merely a governess." He set his glass on a table and took hers to set it down also so he could possess her hands. He bent to kiss her fingertips.

"Adrian—I—perhaps this was not a good idea."

He moved closer, slipping his arm around her. He brushed his lips against her neck and felt her tremble in response. The fresh, woodsy smell of her hair and skin was intoxicating.

"Au contraire, my love. It is an excellent idea. Besides, I have your brother's permission."

She pulled away from him with a startled look in her eyes. "You *what?"*

"Last night I asked for and received Peter's permission to pay my addresses to you."

"Oh, Adrian. Surely you know it is impossible." She reached her hand to caress his cheek, sending desire surging through him. He caught her hand and placed a lingering kiss on her palm.

"No. I know no such thing."

"But the scandal. Even now the *ton* must be feasting on my having served as governess here."

"And tomorrow when Lady So-and-So runs off with her footman, they will savor another dish. It does not signify."

"But it does. Your position with the Foreign Office . . ."

"Is secure. They need me," he said smugly. Then he added, his voice suddenly husky, "And *I* need *you.* I love you. I want to marry you. Please say yes."

"Adrian, I love you, too, but it will not work. Had we met under different circumstances . . ."

He could not endure the pain in her eyes. Clutching her

head gently between his hands, he pressed his lips to hers in a searing, searching, probing kiss that sought to quell all her doubts. Caught up in the intensity of her response, it was some moments before he drew back only far enough to whisper, "You see? Everything else is irrelevant to this."

He would have pulled her closer for another kiss, but she put her fingers against his lips. "What about your family? Your mother will hate the circumstances of our relationship. I cannot believe your father would favor such a match."

Adrian laughed softly. "You are reaching for obstacles where none need exist, my love. Once they understand how much I love you, they will welcome you with open arms. Their own marriage was a love match, you know."

"Oh."

"Aunt Henny liked you. Uncle Philip thought you charming. Caroline was friendly enough tonight, was she not?"

"Yes, but . . ."

"And the most important people in my family absolutely adore you—as do I." He punctuated his words with a bombardment of kisses to her eyes, cheeks, nose, and lips. "Geoffrey and Bess need you as their mother, not their governess. And Anne needs you as well."

"I hate the idea of leaving them—and you," she said softly.

"Then don't." He sensed her yielding. "Besides, you cannot return to the Continent as Peter said you planned. There is going to be war there again. And I had your Lady Mary Kincannon MacGregor investigated. She has been dead these five years and more."

"Are you telling me I have no choice but to marry you?"

"Do you? Do you want a choice?" he asked with a kiss that demonstrated most thoroughly that his children's needs aside, the Marquis of Trenville had his own needs that only she could fulfill.

"No, not at all."

And she gave herself up to an equally thorough response.

ABOUT THE AUTHOR

Wilma Counts lives in Nevada. She is currently working on her third Zebra Regency romance, which will be published in November 2000. Wilma loves hearing from readers and you may write to her c/o Zebra Books. Please include a self-addressed stamped envelope if you wish a response.